HELP!
I SMELL A
MONSTER

JUSTIN DAVIES
ILLUSTRATED BY KIM GEYER

ORCHARD

ORCHARD BOOKS

First published in Great Britain in 2019 by The Watts Publishing Group

1 3 5 7 9 10 8 6 4 2

Text copyright © Justin Davies 2019
Illustrations copyright © Kim Geyer 2019

A CIP catalogue record for this book is available from the British Library.

ISBN 978 1 40835 546 6

Printed and bound in Great Britain by
CPI Group (UK) Ltd, Croydon, CR0 4YY

The paper and board used in this book are made from
wood from responsible sources

MIX
Paper from
responsible sources
FSC® C104740
FSC
www.fsc.org

Orchard Books
An imprint of Hachette Children's Group
Part of The Watts Publishing Group Limited
Carmelite House, 50 Victoria Embankment, London EC4Y 0DZ

An Hachette UK Company
www.hachette.co.uk
www.hachettechildrens.co.uk

CONTENTS

1. TONGUE-TIED

As far as Alice MacAlister knew, there were several ways to open a door, but using your tongue wasn't one of them.

Keys were useful. Doorbells and knockers worked well too. Failing that, banging with your fists often had excellent results, as did yelling through a letterbox. But this!

Alice checked the sign next to the door to make sure she hadn't misread it: **LICK HERE TO ENTER – AUTHORISED VISITORS ONLY** it said, with arrows pointing down to a shiny black screen.

'**Yuk!**' she said. 'That's just weird.'

A sudden gust of cold wind whipped up a vortex of dry leaves around her ankles and she shivered. *Right*, she thought, *screaming through a letterbox isn't going to work, because there isn't a letterbox*. That left fists. She rapped on the door as hard as she could, shouting, **'Uncle Magnus! Hello! Anybody!'**

What was he doing in there? 'Ten minutes, tops,' he'd said as he dumped her in the café above his basement office. But that had been over an hour ago, and now here she was, toes freezing, in front of a door that wouldn't open. This was not a good start to her week in Scotland – a week she'd hoped might be different and exciting and everything her school holidays usually weren't. But now, Alice thought she might as well be back home where nothing ever happened and where holidays were all about being bored with her friends, dreaming of living somewhere where interesting things actually did happen.

She thought about going back up to the café where she'd promised to wait. The friendly barista, Doogie, who Uncle Magnus had said was going to keep an eye on her, would probably make her another **Flaming Hotto Lotto Chocco.** There were still bits of burnt marshmallow stuck in her teeth from the last one. And in the café, she could warm her feet and breathe in the wonderful smells of melting chocolate and just-brewed coffee.

Or, since she was going to get into trouble for sneaking out of the café anyway, and since her uncle had clearly forgotten about her, and since it was important to remind him that he was supposed to be treating her to an exciting holiday in Edinburgh and not working in his office . . . she might as well have another go at opening the door. Even if it was the silliest thing she'd ever done.

Alice rubbed the screen with her sleeve to clean it. Then, poking out her tongue, she leaned forward and gave it a quick dab. Nothing happened. On her second attempt, she made sure to stick out as much tongue as possible so she could lick the screen from bottom to top. She stood back and wiped her lips, trying to get a fishy taste out of her mouth.

Still nothing. Like you could open a door by licking it!

Alice turned to walk back up to the café, but just then, she heard a quiet beep, followed by a click.

'No way!' She pushed the door and – hey presto! – it swung open. Stepping through, she saw that it opened on to a narrow corridor, the walls of which were covered with posters, many with their corners curling inwards.

Central Library.
Tall creature wanted for
high-level book shelving.
Kindly giants only, please.

PHARMACEUTICAL POSITIONS.
WITCHES WANTED.
APPLY WITHIN.

FLYING JOBS
FOR WINGED BEASTS.
GR8 RATES OF PAY.
USUAL BENEFITS.
SORRY, NO PHOENIXES.

Words leaped out at her from other posters as
she made her way towards a door at the far end –
'dragons', **'poltergeists'** and **'yetis'**.

A tingling sensation wriggled up Alice's back.

'What's going on?' she whispered to herself. The frosted glass in the door meant she couldn't see inside, but then she spotted words engraved in the glass:

WELCOME TO

JOBS 4 MONSTERS

Come in!

2. EPIC FAIL

Absolutely one hundred per cent certain that this was a joke, Alice did as the sign instructed and went in.

She found herself standing in what looked like a dentist's waiting room – plastic chairs and a sofa lined three walls, and there were a few low tables covered with books and magazines. They separated the seats from a large desk, which had a sign on it, saying: **Reception. Ring for attention.**

Alice looked for a bell but couldn't see one anywhere. 'Typical,' she muttered, suddenly noticing an odd smell hanging over everything. In fact, there were loads of weird smells – and Alice didn't recognise any of them.

To the side of the desk there was another door. It was closed, but Alice could just make out her uncle's muffled voice. It sounded like he was on the phone – probably making another **VERY IMPORTANT CALL**. *This really isn't fair*, thought Alice. If her uncle had known he was going to be too busy, he should have refused to have her. Not that there'd been any other options . . .

Alice folded her arms and groaned. It was hardly her fault that her mum had had to go away at short notice to some conference during the school holidays. And she couldn't help it if she was terrified of snakes and so couldn't stay with Nana Molly who'd just acquired a pet boa constrictor called Rupert. Great-Grandad Bertie was out of the question, too, because his Jackahuahua, Brutus, was still going strong and Alice's overprotective mum had never let her anywhere near him – or any other dog for that matter.

And she could hardly be blamed for her total phobia of flying, which meant her Aunt Maureen in Spain wasn't an option either. No, Uncle Magnus was something of a last resort. He'd been forced to travel down south to collect her and take her back to Edinburgh on the train, when he clearly didn't have the time.

Alice jumped as the phone started ringing, but nobody rushed in to answer it. She stood in the middle of the room for another minute then threw her satchel on to the sofa and slumped down next to it, sending a mushroom cloud of dust into the air. 'What *is* this place?' she whispered.

Maybe her uncle worked at some sort of theatre agency. Come to think of it, she remembered her mum saying something about her brother Magnus working in recruitment. So that was it! He helped actors find roles as giants and witches and poltergeists. A bit weird, but there was obviously a need for it.

Alice got up and wandered over to a mirror. Somehow, a cobweb had become tangled up in her hair. As she began picking it out, she noticed a sign pinned to the wall above the mirror:

VAMPIRE CHECK
WE CAN SEE YOU,
BUT CAN YOU
SEE YOU?

She looked back at her reflection and blinked. Then she spotted more posters on a noticeboard. They seemed to be job adverts too, like the ones in the corridor:

GHOSTS WANTED
FOR CASTLE HAUNTINGS
(MUST BE IN POSSESSION OF
LICENCE TO THRILL)

SEEKING MERMAIDS
FOR THERAPIST POSITIONS
AT A NEW
AQUATIC WELLNESS CLINIC

NIGHT-TIME SECURITY
GUARD NEEDED AT
MONSTER MEGAMALL —
WOULD SUIT NON-SMOKING
DRAGON

Alice gulped. Was there anything normal in here? Her eyes zipped sideways, landing on a framed photo. It was hard to see what the person in it looked like because someone had drawn on a comedy moustache and glasses in black marker pen, but the brass plaque underneath it was easy to read:

GIDEON DRAGSTORM
MINISTER FOR MONSTERS

Alice took a step back and stumbled into one of the tables, scattering books and magazines across the floor. She bent down and reached for the nearest magazine, nearly dropping it again when she noticed the dragon plastered on the front cover. Its shimmering purple-blue scales looked unbelievably real. **Monsters Weekly**, read Alice. She flipped it open to an article called: **How to keep your scales in peak condition.**

She fumbled it back on the table and grabbed another magazine – **Which Witch: Your monthly consumer guide to cauldrons, spells and broomsticks.** By the time she'd reached for a third – a cookery title called **Bones and Blood** – Alice had to steady herself against the wall, her legs quivering like not-quite-set jelly. It was as if she'd stumbled on to a movie set. But this wasn't a film studio, she was at her uncle's office.

And who would go to this much effort just for a laugh? Alice had to admit, whatever was going on here, the morning had suddenly become much less dull.

The phone ringing for a second time made Alice jump again, knocking over another pile of magazines. Before she had a chance to pick them up, she heard a clattering outside. Someone – or something – was approaching fast.

Alice edged closer to the sofa, her heart beating almost as loudly as the phone was ringing.

'I'm coming! Hold your hippogriffs!' a voice called from the other side of the door.

Then, through the frosted glass, Alice saw a shadow hurtling towards her.

'Och, for goodness sake relax, I'm coming! I'm com— **EOWWWW!**'

The shadow crashed against the door and it burst

open. A blur of long green hair billowed into the reception area. Alice, now wedged in behind the sofa, watched as the figure somersaulted in the air like a gymnast, landing perfectly on top of the desk. The tray they'd been carrying hurtled on towards the far wall, covering it in a tidal wave of coffee and soggy crumbs.

'These stupid boots!' The green-haired person pointed to her purple wellington boots, whilst looking straight at Alice with the brightest blue eyes ever. 'I keep tripping up in them.' She reached down for the still-ringing phone. *'Jobs4Monsters, Miss Pinky speaking. How may I help you?'* She dropped the phone on to the desk and looked back at Alice. 'How rude. They hung up.' Then she leaped off the desk, splashing down in the puddle of brown liquid from the coffee tray.

Alice must have been mesmerised by the green

hair and purple boots, because it was only now that she noticed Miss Pinky was wearing a grinning cat emoji T-shirt, which she'd teamed with a pink mini skirt. It made her own skinny jeans and trainers combo seem a bit boring.

'Let me help you clean that up,' said Alice.

'No way! We can't have a client doing the cleaning – unless you're here for the poop collecting job at the dragon day care centre, in which case, you're hired! LOL!'

'No,' said Alice, wondering if she'd heard correctly. 'I'm not a client.'

Miss Pinky's eyes narrowed to blue slits. 'Not a client? Who are you then?'

Alice laughed nervously. 'Well, for a start, I'm only eleven. Too young to work.'

Miss Pinky leaned in for a closer look. It was only now that Alice noticed the white, cat-like whiskers on her face.

'If you're too young to work, what are you doing in an employment agency?'

'I . . . I came with Magnus,' Alice stuttered, trying not to stare at the whiskers.

'Och, well, why didn't you say?' Miss Pinky's eyes widened and then she slapped her head. 'Doh! I know who you are. With hair as ginger as that, you must be a MacAlister. You're Alice!'

Alice nodded. 'And your name's Miss Pinky?'

'That's me!' She grabbed Alice's hand and shook it vigorously before turning her attention to her mobile.

'Er, we should really clean that up.' Alice pointed to the pool of coffee Miss Pinky was still standing in.

'Aye . . . just a minute . . . need to update my status. That was such an epic fail with the coffee.' She tapped away at her phone frantically. 'Right, that's done. It should get me some new followers.' She looked at the floor. 'What a mess! Why didn't you say? Magnus will go bananas.' The receptionist swept her long hair back into a ponytail (it matched her green eyebrows perfectly, Alice noticed), and stepped over to a door marked 'Staff Only', almost tripping in her boots again.

'Maybe you should take them off?' Alice suggested.

Miss Pinky grabbed a mop and bucket from behind the door. 'Can't. I have to keep them on. People get totally freaked otherwise.'

'I'm sure your feet aren't that bad,' said Alice.

'Paws,' said Miss Pinky.

'What do you mean, "paws"?' asked Alice.

'I have paws,' explained Miss Pinky, 'not feet.'

'Oh! But your hands are, you know, hands. Aren't they?'

The receptionist held her hands up. 'Yes,' she

said. 'They say you can tell a lot about someone by their hands. But in my case, they only tell half the story.'

Alice stared at Miss Pinky. Was it rude to ask to see someone's paws? Because despite being a bit freaked out, she really wanted to see them.

'I'll show you if you like,' said Miss Pinky. 'As long as you promise not to go all crazy on me and run out screaming your wee head off.'

'I promise.'

Miss Pinky sat on her chair and tugged off her boots, revealing very black and very furry paws, just like a cat's.

Alice looked up at Miss Pinky's whiskers, then she looked around the room – at the bizarre posters and the magazines and the vampire-check mirror. 'You're not, um, human, are you?'

Miss Pinky shrieked. 'As if!'

'What *are* you then?'

'I'm a splicer,' said Miss Pinky. 'Half one creature, half another. In my case, part mermaid, part cait sith.'

Alice shook her head. 'Never heard of a cait . . . whatever you just said.'

'Cait sith,' said Miss Pinky. 'It's a giant monster cat. Pretty random mix, isn't it?' She stood blinking at Alice. 'You're not scared of cats, are you?'

Alice shook her head. 'It's dogs and snakes I'm terrified of.'

'Phew!' Miss Pinky fanned herself with a piece of paper.

Alice took a deep breath. 'So, you're a . . . monster, then?'

Miss Pinky nodded. 'Yes, Alice. I am a monster.'

'And you're also this place's receptionist,' said Magnus, who'd appeared in the doorway leading to his office. 'So you'd better start doing some receptioning.'

'That's not even a word,' said Miss Pinky.

'It is now. And unless you start work immediately, you will no longer be in the running for EMPLOYEE OF THE WEEK.'

Miss Pinky gasped. 'But I'm your only employee! I'm always the winner!'

Magnus sighed. 'You can only win if you do some work.'

Miss Pinky pouted and began tapping away on her phone.

'And you can start by putting that thing away,' said Magnus, who turned to face Alice. She wished he hadn't, because his eyes had narrowed into a really angry frown. 'Right. What are you doing here and how did you get in?'

'Oh yeah,' said Miss Pinky, looking up. 'I was going

to ask her that.'

They both stared at Alice. 'I was bored,' she said. 'I thought you'd forgotten about me, so I came to find you.'

'But how did you manage to get in?' asked Magnus.

Alice could feel herself going red; this was turning into a proper police interrogation. 'I used that pad thing.'

'The TRS let YOU in?' Miss Pinky leaped up from her desk and was hopping from paw to paw.

'The what?' asked Alice.

'The Tongue Recognition System,' said Miss Pinky. 'It's only supposed to let in—'

'Authorised people,' said Magnus, interrupting Miss Pinky. 'It must be broken. Did you lick it?'

'Yes,' said Alice.

'I KNEW I could taste something!' said Miss Pinky. 'Have you had one of Doogie's hotto choccos?'

Alice nodded, wrinkling her nose. *Maybe*, she thought, *I should have wiped the TRS after licking it as well!*

'Excellent choice,' said Miss Pinky. 'They're the best.'

Magnus cleared his throat. 'I expect you have some questions about all this,' he said.

'About a million,' said Alice.

'Not sure there's time to answer that many,' said Magnus. 'How about just asking the one question you really want answered?'

Alice didn't need to think twice. 'Is all this for real? Do monsters actually exist?'

'Technically,' said Magnus, smiling, 'that's two questions. But the answer's yes to both.'

'Wow.' Alice felt a tingle begin to work its way up her back – the sort she got when she woke up and remembered it was Christmas Day.

'Jeepers, Magnus!' cried Miss Pinky. 'No wonder

Alice has never been to visit before. She doesn't know!'

Magnus shrugged. 'I was the last resort. The bottom of Alice's mum's list. To be called on only in dire emergencies.'

Miss Pinky laughed. 'That's hardly surprising considering you're a—'

'Manager of a recruitment agency for monsters,' interrupted Magnus. 'Yes, thank you, Miss Pinky. There's lots of things Alice doesn't know about me, and that's one of them.'

Alice stared at her uncle. 'Like what? What else?'

Magnus turned red. He ran his hand through his hair. Was it possible for hair to blush? His seemed to have gone even redder than it already was. 'If I told you, I'd have to kill you. HA! Only joking! And now, Miss Pinky, perhaps you would like to do some work please. You're late enough as it is this morning.'

'I couldn't help it. There was a gigantical queue upstairs at Monsters' Munch.' She turned to Alice. 'Doogie's Triple Grande Double Cream Mocha Chocca Latte is awesome. Especially with some fish sauce on top.'

'Yuk!'

'Oh no,' said Miss Pinky, 'they're really good. In fact, I think I'll nip upstairs to get another one.'

'Absolutely not,' said Magnus, as the phone started ringing again. 'The only place you're going is back to work. You can start by answering that.'

'So not fair,' mumbled Miss Pinky, slouching back to her desk and grabbing the phone. 'Good morning, Jobs4Monsters, Miss Pinky speaking. How may I help you? Yes . . . I see . . . oh dear . . . oh no . . . that's terrible. Just a moment.' She held the phone out to Magnus. ***'It's Balmoral Castle,'*** she said. ***'The cyclops is on the loose.'***

3. WEIRD WILD WEB

The atmosphere in Jobs4Monsters suddenly changed. The news from the castle sent both its staff into a tizzy. Magnus couldn't seem to stop pacing around, pulling at tufts of his hair, whilst Miss Pinky moved papers from one side of her desk to the other, and back again.

'We're not actually talking about a real cyclops, are we?' asked Alice. 'Like, from Greek myths?'

'Yes,' said Magnus, 'an actual cyclops.'

Alice had learned about Greek legends the year before in school. Some of the creatures had razor-sharp claws and teeth and enough heads to eat an entire netball team in one go, but she couldn't remember much about the cyclops.

'I thought those stories were just stories,' she said, 'you know . . . made up.'

Magnus shook his head. 'The stories might be made up,' he said, 'but the creatures are real enough.'

'Let me get this right,' said Alice. 'Monsters are real?'

'Yes,' said Magnus.

'And they're out there right now?'

'She's catching on,' said Miss Pinky.

'And,' continued Alice, 'you help these . . . er . . . monsters find jobs.'

'That's it,' said Magnus.

'Do they come here to be interviewed?' asked Alice, wondering if the bizarre odours she'd smelled came from real-life monsters.

'Only some monsters are allowed to come here,' explained Magnus. 'We make other arrangements for the rest. Isn't that right, Miss Pinky?'

'Absolutely. At Jobs4Monsters we are happy to provide videoconferencing or home visits.' Miss Pinky grabbed a leaflet from a pile on her desk. 'Look! We'll do mountains, caves, the bottom of lochs. Our motto is, "If you promise not to eat us, we'll visit so you can meet us!"'

'It's catchy,' said Alice. 'But why do monsters need jobs? Can't they just go around being, you know, monsters?'

Miss Pinky squealed with laughter. 'How do you think I buy my fabulous clothes?' She stepped out from behind the desk and performed a catwalk twirl. 'Monsters like all the things humans do,' she said, sitting down again. 'Phones, movies, pizzas, muffins, coffee . . .'

Magnus nodded in agreement. 'Miss Pinky's right,' he said, 'monsters need money too. Which means they need jobs.'

Alice's brain was still playing catch-up with the facts bombarding her. 'Why doesn't everyone know about it? I've never seen any monsters.'

'Lots of them don't look any different from us, Alice,' said Magnus.

'Or not much,' said Miss Pinky, licking a whisker.

'Anyway,' said Magnus, 'it's against the law for humans to know about monsters.'

Alice stared at her uncle. This was getting crazy. 'I've never heard of a law like that.'

'That's kind of the point,' said Miss Pinky, leafing through a massive leather-bound book she'd heaved off a shelf behind her desk. 'Here you are . . . Monster Integration Act, section five, subsection forty-eight, paragraph nine:

No monster shall be visible to humans if:

a) they cannot alter their physical appearance;

b) they are unable to communicate in a human language;

c) they cannot contain their monster tendencies.

Alice suddenly realised she was doing an Oscar-worthy impression of a fish out of water. Another trillion questions zoomed around her head as she gasped for air.

'So, you're telling me there are loads of dangerous monsters hidden out there that no one knows about?'

Magnus sighed. 'Yes.'

Alice stared at her uncle. 'How come you know? You're a human.'

'Well . . . uh . . . I have special . . . Ministry of

Monsters clearance,' Magnus told her.

'So, *some* humans do know about monsters?' asked Alice.

Magnus nodded. 'Yes, but very few. They're mostly at the top level of government . . . and . . . um . . . me.'

'Does my mum know?'

Miss Pinky laughed. 'Of course she does! Her brother's a—'

Magnus coughed. 'Her brother is a manager at Jobs4Monsters. Thank you, Miss Pinky.' He threw a glare-bomb at the receptionist – the sort Alice might use when she next saw her mum. How could her own mother not share something as amazing as this?

As if her uncle had guessed what she'd been thinking, he came over and put an arm around Alice. 'She wasn't allowed to tell you,' he explained, 'it's against the law.'

Miss Pinky flicked through a couple more pages of the book. 'Section six, subsection twenty-two, paragraph seven:

Humans with knowledge of monsters may not tell another human.

'So,' said Alice, 'how does the royal family keep this huge giant a secret?'

'Easy,' said Magnus. 'They *only* employ monsters at their Scottish castle.' He sighed and shook his head. 'Poor Polyphemus.'

'Is that the cyclops's name?' asked Alice.

'Yes,' said Magnus. 'He's a chef, and a very good one at that.'

'Not bad for a one-eyed giant,' said Miss Pinky.

Alice looked at Miss Pinky. 'He only has one eye?'

Magnus tutted. 'Didn't you study Greek mythology at school?'

'We did,' said Alice, 'but it looks like they left some important stuff out of the lessons.' *Just wait until I tell my friends what our school books missed out*, she thought, before suddenly remembering the Monster Act. She was going to have to keep all this secret!

'Look,' said Magnus, 'I know you've got tons of questions, and there's loads I should probably try and explain, but right now we need to concentrate on the missing cyclops. When the Ministry of Monsters hears about his disappearance, they'll be on the case before you know it. Any monsters in Category Four or above need special permission to leave their designated area. Polyphemus is in Category Five and he didn't have ministry clearance. He'll end up in

MonsterMax for this.'

Miss Pinky shuddered. 'It's supposed to be awful. Full of the nastiest, meanest, most dangerous monster prisoners.'

'But recently, the new minister's been sending monsters there for the smallest crimes,' said Magnus. 'I heard he sentenced a fairy to six months for not having a pilot's licence.' He pointed to the photo of Gideon Dragstorm. 'Our esteemed minister is a real stickler for the rules.'

Miss Pinky laughed from behind her computer. 'That's putting it nicely,' she screeched. 'You should see what they call him on the web!'

'Hold on!' Alice ran over to the desk and leaned over Miss Pinky's shoulder. 'I've never seen anything about monsters online.'

'That, young Alice,' said Miss Pinky, 'is because it's not on *your* web. It's on *ours*. THE WEIRD WILD WEB.'

'No way!' cried Alice. 'There's an internet just for monsters!'

Miss Pinky beamed. 'Like, duh! We've got the lot: FierceBook, Screecher, Snapjaw, Monstagram.' The receptionist flicked a switch and the screen went blank. 'But I'll be arrested if I let you see it. Monsters Act, section something or other, subsection blah, blah, blah.'

Alice stared at the blank screen for a second. 'It's not like it's a secret any more,' she muttered.

'I'll show you when your uncle's not watching,' Miss Pinky whispered.

'It doesn't matter what people say about him,' said Magnus. 'If Dragstorm finds out we can't keep track of a monster like Polyphemus, he'll close us down. We're behind with our paperwork as it is. Since he became minister, the department's tripled the amount of forms we have to fill in. Look at my desk!' Alice peered into Magnus's office, where his desk was hidden under an avalanche of files and folders.

'It's so unfair,' moaned Miss Pinky. 'This is the best job I've ever had.'

'It's the *only* job you've ever had,' Magnus said wryly.

'I don't get it,' said Alice. 'Isn't this Dragstorm guy supposed to be on your side? I mean, he is a monster too, isn't he?'

Miss Pinky tapped on her phone and held it out for Alice to see. 'He's one of these.'

Alice looked at the image: the top half of the creature looked human, apart from two shiny horns poking out through its thick curly hair like broom handles. But the bottom half was all furry, with sheep-like hooves. 'What is that?' she asked.

'A faun,' said Miss Pinky. 'They're usually super

friendly and super kind. Doogie upstairs is one too.'

'Is he? I didn't notice anything,' said Alice.

'He hides his horns under his beanie,' said Miss Pinky, 'and he always wears long trousers.' She winked. 'He's super good-looking, isn't he, Magnus?'

Magnus suddenly became flustered and red in the cheeks. 'He wasn't super good at keeping an eye on Alice.'

Alice bit her bottom lip. Now she could feel herself blushing. 'I sort of crept out when he wasn't looking. Sorry.'

Magnus shrugged. 'I shouldn't have left you there for so long,' he said, 'but I was busy on the phone.'

'Doesn't matter,' said Alice, wondering if she'd have discovered any of this if she'd stayed in the café. 'I just don't get why this Dragstorm is being so horrid.'

'I reckon he's jealous of other monsters,' said

Magnus, 'and their powers. In Monster Top Trumps, he's the card nobody wants!'

'Exactly!' said Miss Pinky. 'Fauns wouldn't last long in a monster death match, would they? You can't defeat a dragon or slay a sea serpent by being sweet and playing the pan pipes.'

Suddenly, Magnus clutched his head in both hands. 'The cyclops!' He turned to Alice. 'I'm really sorry but your holiday will have to wait. I need to make some more calls in my office. Would you mind staying here with Miss Pinky?'

Mind! thought Alice. *As if!* Life had just become about a gazillion times more interesting.

'I suppose I could manage,' she said, failing to hide the smile spreading rapidly over her face.

'Thanks,' said Magnus. 'And Miss Pinky, don't forget we've a banshee coming in today. Can you deal with her?'

'A banshee?' Alice looked at her uncle and Miss Pinky. 'Are they, you know, dangerous?'

'Can be,' said Miss Pinky, 'if you upset them.'

Magnus hesitated at his office door. 'Banshee bedlam is the last thing we need today, Miss Pinky. I'm sure Alice would prefer to make it to teatime in one piece.'

Alice gulped. There was no way she wanted to be torn in two by a banshee. Or by anything!

4. CAUTION ➡ LOW FLYING MONSTER!

The second Magnus had disappeared into his office, Miss Pinky grabbed Alice's arm. 'Let's go for coffee,' she said.

'But what about the banshee?' asked Alice. 'And how come you're allowed to be seen anyway? You've got whiskers!'

'I pretend they're body art,' said Miss Pinky. 'I've seen way weirder stuff on humans. Let's go – but be quiet; we don't want Magnus knowing we're sneaking out.'

Alice walked to the sofa to pick up her satchel.

'Shhh! Stop stomping about!' whispered Miss Pinky.

'Relax, he doesn't have bionic ears,' laughed Alice.

'Believe me,' said Miss Pinky, tiptoeing towards the door, 'your uncle can hear vampires grinding their teeth through a brick wall. Come on! Last one there's a stinky human!'

Ten minutes later, they were back outside the Jobs4Monsters entrance, balancing gigantic toffee muffins on top of their drinks. Alice had become almost giddy with the delicious aroma of freshly baked muffins in the café, and Miss Pinky had insisted she try one. But now all Alice could smell was the reek of the fish sauce Doogie had squirted on top of Miss Pinky's Triple Grande Double Cream Mocha Chocca Latte. Luckily, Alice had stopped him before he'd added some to her second blazing mallow hot chocolate of the day.

Miss Pinky tossed her green ponytail over her shoulder. She'd been swishing it all over the place whilst Doogie had made their drinks in a totally obvious effort to catch his eye. 'Don't know why I bothered,' she grumbled, 'your uncle's more his type.' She sighed and handed Alice her coffee to hold. 'OK, you lick, I'll push.'

As soon as they were in the corridor, Alice could hear something going on inside the reception area. 'Banshees,' she said, 'they're not, you know, *really* dangerous, are they?'

'Oh no,' said Miss Pinky, taking back her coffee, 'not unless they get angry. Then it's mega chaos.'

'Oh . . .' said Alice, as a wailing sound reverberated

through the door. It was a bit like a fire engine siren, only at double speed. 'Something's not right.' She tried to squeeze back out past Miss Pinky. 'Better not go in.'

'Nonsense, it's just the banshee. She must be early,' said Miss Pinky. 'Nothing to worry about. Everything's purrfectly normal. But perhaps we shouldn't keep her waiting any longer.'

Alice felt her tummy somersault. 'After you, then.'

'No. You first.'

'No!' Alice shook her head. 'You.'

Miss Pinky snarled. 'YOU!'

'YOU!' yelled Alice, wondering if she should be frightened of Miss Pinky. She was a monster, after all.

'I don't want to,' moaned the receptionist.

'But I don't even work here.'

Miss Pinky growled.

'Well, it's true,' said Alice. 'You're the one who

works here, not me.'

Miss Pinky growled again, revealing *very* sharp teeth.

Woah! thought Alice. It looked like she didn't have a choice. *OK, you can do this.* She took a couple of deep breaths and pushed open the door.

Instantly she was pinned against the wall by a whirring, screaming blur. It whizzed around the reception like out-of-control helicopter rotors.

"*AAAIIIEEEE!*"

Alice's hot chocolate was whipped out of her hand by the creature's hair. It flew across the room and splattered on the wall. Through the banshee's high-speed spinning, Alice caught sight of Miss Pinky, crawling on her paws and hands towards the sofa.

Alice ducked down and commando-crawled across the floor, squeezing behind the sofa after Miss Pinky, who yelped. 'Och! That was my paw!'

'Sorry!' yelled Alice over the din, shoving Miss Pinky along to make room.

Wriggling around to peek out, Alice saw the banshee bounce off a wall and ricochet into Magnus, who had emerged from his office. He went flying across the room, fell over a chair and landed on the sofa, legs akimbo, arms askew. Alice heard several springs take the opportunity to uncoil themselves, and judging by his yelps, some of them had sprung up into her uncle.

'Are you all right?' Alice peered over the sofa arm, picking up Magnus's wallet and keys, which had landed on the floor next to her.

'Apart from being attacked by a banshee, you mean?' he shouted.

'AAAIIIEEEE! AAAIIIEEEEEEE! AAAIIIEEEEEEEEEEE! IS ANYBODY HERE?'

'Will you please **chill out?'** yelled Miss Pinky.

The banshee came to a sudden stop; a perfect end-of-routine spin that Alice had never achieved in hundreds of skating lessons.

'Och, there you are,' said the banshee, smoothing down her curly white hair. 'Why didn't you say?'

Alice crept out from behind the sofa. The banshee's dark eyes stared in a glazed-over, just-been-hypnotised kind of way. Apart from that, she looked like a normal old lady in her boring straight skirt and blouse combo. Even so, Alice didn't want to get too close.

Miss Pinky skipped over to her desk and tapped on her keyboard. 'Are you Mildred Meekly?'

'Aye, hen. That's me.'

'It says here,' said Miss Pinky, reading her screen, 'that we recently found you employment in the Edinburgh Children's Library as a "Quiet-Time Supervisor".'

'Aye, that you did,' said Mildred. 'It didn't work out. They said I wasn't suited to the subdued environment. I can't imagine what they meant by that.'

'And now you're here for the Trainee Therapist post at the Sea of Tranquillity Day Spa. Is that correct?'

'Aye. Your online job finder matched me up with it.'

Miss Pinky beamed. 'That's our newest initiative,' she said, turning to Alice. 'The monsters input their skills, experience and personality traits, then the programme finds them the perfect position.'

Alice peered at Miss Pinky's screen. 'It also

matched her with a vacancy at Little Tykes Day Nursery.' She glanced over to the banshee, who was manically twirling her hair round her fingers. 'Are you sure your programme works properly?'

Miss Pinky licked a whisker. 'Perhaps it needs a tweak or two,' she said.

'I'll say,' said Magnus, taking Mildred's arm and steering her to the entrance. 'I think you'd better come back another time. Sorry for the inconvenience.'

Mildred's face had turned a deep shade of purple and it looked like she was building up to another whirlwind. Magnus quickly opened the door and nudged the banshee out. 'Cheerio!' he called, slamming the door shut and locking it.

He looked around the reception and tutted. 'This will have to be cleaned up,' he said, 'and your online job finder needs fixing too, Miss Pinky. Meanwhile,

I'll try to track down the missing cyclops.' Magnus disappeared into his office, leaving Alice and Miss Pinky to deal with the mess.

'Phew!' said Miss Pinky. 'That was close!'

'Close?' laughed Alice. 'We nearly got our heads knocked off by a ballistic banshee!'

'Double LOL,' said Miss Pinky, grabbing her phone. 'Now if you'll excuse me, my Monstagram followers need updating.'

Alice grabbed a mop and began cleaning up their spilt drinks, whilst Miss Pinky messed around with her phone. Normally, she would have been a bit miffed at being dumped with the cleaning but having survived an encounter with an out-of-control banshee, Alice was on a high. This was easily the most thrilling start to a school holiday she'd ever had.

When the office phone rang again, Miss Pinky

didn't seem to notice; she was totally absorbed by her mobile, which had been pinging almost constantly.

'Miss Pinky, the phone,' Alice called.

'What?' Miss Pinky said, without looking up.

'The phone. It's ringing. Don't you think you should answer it?'

Miss Pinky tutted. 'So annoying, I'm nearly at five thousand Monstagram followers.' She threw down her mobile and lunged for the office phone. 'Jobs4Monsters, Miss Pinky speaking. How may I help you? . . . Oh, it's you again . . . OK . . . Putting you through now.' Miss Pinky pulled a face and pushed a button. 'Magnus, sorry to interrupt, but it's the castle again . . . They're insisting.'

A few minutes later, Magnus reappeared, his face lined with concern and his hair wild. 'This cyclops business is worse than we thought. It's a downright disaster. It's a complete calamity. It's—'

'An epic fail?' suggested Miss Pinky.

'NOBODY says that any more,' said Magnus, 'but yes, that's about the sum of it.'

Miss Pinky pursed her lips. 'Well, the castle certainly seems incredibly stressed about it.'

'With reason, Miss Pinky. This weekend they're supposed to be hosting the finals of the annual Royal Bake Off. The British royals are one bake away from a record thirty consecutive wins.' Magnus sat down, his head in his hands. 'Without Polyphemus, they don't stand a chance.'

'Wait a minute,' said Alice, trying to keep up, 'there's a Royal Bake Off? I've never seen that on the TV.'

Miss Pinky shrieked with laughter. 'It's not even on *our* TV, Alice! And yes, before you ask, we have our own television shows too.'

'Never mind that,' said Magnus, sounding frustrated. 'What about the cyclops? He's never left the castle on his own.'

'Why not?' asked Alice.

Miss Pinky purred slightly. 'Well, he's blind in one eye, for a start.'

'I thought he only had one eye,' said Alice.

'He does. And he's completely blind in it.'

'I don't get it,' said Magnus. 'How can you lose a creature like Polyphemus? You couldn't exactly miss him lumbering round the castle grounds. And he wouldn't get far unaided.'

'And no one's seen him at all?' asked Alice.

'Nope. His wife is very concerned.'

Poor Mrs Cyclops, thought Alice, picturing a giant lady crying her one big eye out into a sheet-sized handkerchief.

'He just wouldn't up and leave like that,' said Magnus. 'I've known him for years. He's one of our oldest and most reliable clients.'

'Maybe he just fancied a break,' said Alice.

'No chance,' said Magnus. 'He knows what the Monster Act says about his category: *stay in place or face arrest*. They'll probably arrest me too. Dragstorm will want to make an example of me.' He hid his face in his hands. 'The minister will shut us down. I might never work again. I could end up in MonsterMax for years!'

Miss Pinky pointed to Magnus. 'Alice, may I present your uncle, the Drama Queen!'

Alice laughed. 'So, you don't think it's that serious?'

Miss Pinky's eyes widened. 'Oh, yes. It is that serious. In fact, I smell an epically big rat.'

'What do you mean, Miss Pinky?' asked Magnus.

'Well, it's totally obvious: Polyphemus must have been taken against his will.'

Alice gasped. 'Kidnapped?'

'No,' said Miss Pinky. **'MONSTERNAPPED!'**

5. OMG!

'Right, that's it!' said Magnus. 'I'm calling an emergency staff meeting.'

'Let me check my diary,' said Miss Pinky. 'Hmm . . . I'm pretty busy.'

'Are you busy right now?' asked Magnus.

'Yes,' said Miss Pinky. 'I'm busy checking my diary.'

Magnus groaned. 'My office, Miss Pinky. Pronto!' He headed out of the reception, stumbling over a thick book that must have been knocked to the floor by Mildred. He picked it up and brushed it off. 'Ah, the *OMG*!'

'The what?' asked Alice.

'*The Official Monster Guide*,' explained Magnus. 'It's published by the ministry. We'd be lost without it.' He handed it to Alice. 'Why don't you take a look while we're in our meeting?'

As soon as he and Miss Pinky had disappeared into his office, Alice began flicking through the guide. It seemed to be a type of A to Z of monsters, with pictures of all sorts of creatures and information about each one on the opposite page. She stopped at a picture of someone who looked identical to Mildred.

BANSHEE

CATEGORY:	**2**
AVERAGE LIFE SPAN:	**107 YEARS**
HUMAN INTEGRATION:	**YES**
SKILLS: SHRIEKING; HIGH-VELOCITY SPINNING	
RESTRICTIONS:	**NO PUBLIC CONSUMPTION OF CAFFEINE OR HIGH-ENERGY DRINKS**
DANGER RATING:	**LOW-MEDIUM**

Alice turned the pages until she came to the 'Cs'. She gasped when she spotted a picture of a truly terrifying – not to mention ugly – one-eyed giant.

CYCLOPS

CATEGORY:	**5**
AVERAGE LIFE SPAN:	**UNKNOWN**
HUMAN INTEGRATION:	**NO** (EXCEPTIONS: ROYALTY)
SKILLS:	**WEIGHTLIFTING; ROCK-CRUSHING; CAKE-BAKING**
RESTRICTIONS:	**MUST REMAIN IN DESIGNATED MONSTER ZONES**
DANGER RATING:	**EXTREME**

This was great! It was like taking a crash course in monsters. Alice quickly thumbed through to 'F'.

FAUN		
CATEGORY:		1
AVERAGE LIFE SPAN:		67 YEARS
HUMAN INTEGRATION:	YES (SEE RESTRICTIONS)	
SKILLS:	PAN PIPES; MOUNTAIN-CLIMBING	
RESTRICTIONS:	MUST COVER HORNS AND HOOVES IN HUMAN COMPANY	
DANGER RATING:		ZERO

Alice studied the picture of the half-goat creature. She couldn't believe that the guy serving cappuccinos upstairs was one, too. He looked nothing like a monster. Maybe that was why fauns were in the lowest category. Alice was about to check out some other monsters when Magnus and Miss Pinky came back in.

'Grab your coat,' said her uncle. 'We're heading north.'

'Where to?' asked Alice.

'Balmoral Castle, of course.'

'Right now?'

'Yes,' said Magnus. 'We're going to help them find their cyclops.' He looked at her. 'I'm sorry about all this. It's not quite what you expected to be doing on your holiday, is it?'

Alice laughed. 'No, not really. But it's probably just as well. You didn't actually have anything planned, did you?'

Magnus bit his bottom lip and shrugged. 'Look,' he said, 'if searching for a missing cyclops isn't exciting, I don't know what is. How about it?'

Miss Pinky grumbled and folded her arms firmly across her chest. 'It's so unfair that Alice gets to do all the exciting stuff and I have to stay behind.'

Magnus walked over to Miss Pinky. 'I'm leaving you in charge, so if you can try and stay at your desk and out of Monsters' Munch, I'd appreciate it.'

There was something Alice still didn't get. 'Isn't this something the ministry should be dealing with?'

'No way,' said Magnus, 'if the ministry gets involved, Their Majesties will have to be told. They don't know Polyphemus is missing yet, and the staff don't want to worry them. Anyway, I think they trust the minister about as much as we do.'

'Which is less than not at all,' said Miss Pinky.

'The royals will return to the castle in time for the bake off on Saturday,' said Magnus, heading for the entrance. 'So we've got until then to get him back.'

Alice grabbed her satchel and followed Magnus to the door. 'Is it OK if I bring this?' she asked, holding up the *OMG*.

'Excellent idea,' said Magnus, 'you can do some research on the way.'

'Good luck!' cried Miss Pinky.

'Thank you,' said Magnus. 'We'll need it because

if Dragstorm hears about this, I'll be cleaning out the toilets in MonsterMax by this time next week.'

Alice dozed on and off during the long drive to the castle. At one point she was jolted awake from a dream in which a gigantic, one-eyed cat was trying to lap her up out of a paddling pool with its mattress-sized tongue.

She shook the image out of her head and began thumbing through the *OMG*, stopping when she came to a picture of a giant, scary-looking black cat.

'You wouldn't want one of them in your lap,' said Alice.

'One of what?'

Alice showed Magnus the picture.

'Ah, a cait sith,' he said. 'They're very rare these days.'

Alice read the entry opposite the freaky picture.

CAIT SITH		
CATEGORY:		**4**
AVERAGE LIFE SPAN:		**25 YEARS**
HUMAN INTEGRATION:		**NO**
SKILLS:	**POUNCING AT PREY; LEAPING AND LANDING ON THEIR PAWS**	
RESTRICTIONS:	**MONSTER ZONES ONLY**	
DANGER RATING:		**HIGH**

'Miss Pinky's not much like one of these,' said Alice.

'Thankfully,' said Magnus. 'Why don't you look up "mermaid"?'

Alice turned to the 'Ms' and quickly located a

picture of a stunningly beautiful mermaid with shiny green hair and a tail the colour of a tropical ocean.

MERMAID		
CATEGORY:		**2**
AVERAGE LIFE SPAN:		**168 YEARS**
HUMAN INTEGRATION:		**NOT ADVISED**
SKILLS:		**SWIMMING; SINGING; LURING MEN TO THEIR DOOM**
RESTRICTIONS:		**NO SWIMMING NEAR POPULAR BEACHES**
DANGER RATING:		**LOW-MEDIUM**

'Wow!' said Alice. 'I didn't know mermaids were dangerous. Miss Pinky's not, is she?'

'The only thing she's a danger to is a muffin,' said Magnus. 'I have to say, Alice, I'm surprised you're not freaking out about all this.'

'Why?'

'Well,' said Magnus, 'with all your phobias, I thought you'd be terrified of everything. But you seem to be dealing with the whole monster thing OK.'

Alice thought about it and shrugged. 'You can't have a phobia about something you never knew existed, can you?'

'I suppose not,' said Magnus. 'But I still don't see how dogs and snakes are more frightening than a banshee gone berserk.'

'I don't know either,' said Alice. 'Maybe if Mum ever let me near a dog, I'd be OK with them.'

'You've never been near a dog?' asked Magnus, looking confused.

'No,' said Alice. 'Mum says they're not to be trusted. Apparently, they used to try and get in my pram when I was a baby, but I don't remember.' She peered out of the window. They were in the middle of nowhere, with craggy mountains and deep valleys all around. 'And nobody likes snakes, do they?'

'I do,' said Magnus. 'Sometimes all you have to do to get over a phobia is face up to it.'

Alice laughed. 'I suppose,' she said. She looked at her uncle. 'But that doesn't mean I want to stroke a snake, OK?'

'Fine,' said Magnus, stopping the car by an imposing metal gate. 'I just think everyone should try everything once. Anyway, we're here.' He leaned out of the window to press a buzzer and spoke into the intercom. The gates swung open. 'Here goes! The MacAlisters at Balmoral Castle. Grandad Bertie always said the family would come good in the end!'

6. SNAKES ON THE BRAIN

They followed the driveway around the front of the castle, then down the side, heading, as instructed, for the kitchens. Magnus did his best to avoid the speed bumps, but it still felt like a bone-shaker ride at the fairground.

'I feel like we should be in a Rolls-Royce, or something,' said Alice, leaning forward to run her finger through the dust on the dashboard. 'Or something clean, at least.'

Magnus tapped the steering wheel. 'Nothing wrong with this old thing.'

'Yeah right.' Alice waved a hand in front of her

nose. 'Apart from the stink of prawn cocktail crisps and jelly babies.'

Magnus leaned across to open the glove box, which was stuffed with crisps and bags of jelly babies. 'That just happens to be my favourite snack. How did you guess?'

'It's funny,' said Alice. 'I've always been able to sniff things out.'

'Really? That's interesting,' said Magnus, glancing over at her.

It's not going to win me a TV talent show, thought Alice, turning her attention to the castle. Through the teeming rain, she caught glimpses of shadowy turrets and dark windows. In the fading light, it looked a bit creepy.

'We're meeting the housekeeper, Mrs Stuart,' said Magnus. 'Watch out – they say she's a complete dragon.'

'A dragon!' Alice grabbed the guide again and started flicking through the 'Ds'.

Magnus laughed. 'Don't panic, she's not an actual dragon. Just acts like one. No, Mrs Stuart is a splicer, like Miss Pinky. Look out for someone who's part goblin and part ghost.'

'OK,' said Alice, although she couldn't help thinking if this Mrs Stuart was more ghost than goblin, they might not be able to see her at all.

They continued around the castle, driving through a stone archway into a gravelled courtyard.

Alice spotted a short and stout creature wearing a tartan skirt and an angry scowl, standing under a dripping wooden porch. The rain also dripped off the end of her long, shiny nose.

'You're late,' she snapped, as they dashed out of the car.

'You must be Mrs Stuart.' Magnus offered his

hand, which the wrinkled-faced goblin-ghost refused
to shake.

'Aye, that is my name.' The grey hair sprouting
from the housekeeper's pointy
ears bristled like an angry
squirrel's tail.

'May I present my
niece, Alice?' continued
Magnus.

'If you insist,' said Mrs
Stuart, sneering up at Alice
along the length of her nose.

If Alice had been posting a
review on TripAdvisor, Balmoral
Castle would be getting zero stars
for 'welcome'. Judging by the
putrid stink of twice-boiled sprouts
coming from somewhere inside,

they wouldn't be scoring much under 'food' either.

'I've prepared supper,' said Mrs Stuart, as she led them down a dark passageway, 'although I doubt there is enough for two. I wasn't expecting a tour group.'

'Whatever that smell is,' whispered Alice, 'I'm not eating it.'

Magnus turned to Alice. 'What smell?'

'Keep up! Keep up!' barked Mrs Stuart, who, despite her short goblin legs, had raced on ahead. The housekeeper suddenly vanished, then reappeared a split second later about ten steps further on. 'Here we are,' she said, before gliding through a door on the left.

'She doesn't hang about, does she?' said Magnus, turning the handle and holding the door open.

Alice found herself in a gigantic kitchen looking out on to another courtyard. She gazed round at the massive range cooker that took up most of the back wall, and the vast wooden table in the middle of the room. Every inch of wall space was taken up with shelves of china cups, teapots, plates and egg cups decorated with pictures of the royal family.

'Pay attention please,' snapped Mrs Stuart, reaching up to take the lid off a large pan on the cooker. A waft of gut-churning, mushy veg pong filled the kitchen.

'Yuk! I can smell it now,' whispered Magnus.

The housekeeper clattered the pan lid back in place. 'Needs boiling for longer,' she said, 'but I'm far too busy to wait until it's ready.' She glared up at them for a moment. 'Medusa will be with you shortly, so she can serve your supper. Wait here and don't go wandering off.' With that, she bustled over to the door and melted through it.

Alice stared at the door. 'She's very rude.'

'I did warn you,' said Magnus.

'True,' said Alice. 'Who's Medusa?'

'She's the cyclops's wife,' explained Magnus. 'There's a couple of things I should probably tell you about her.'

'Like what?' asked Alice, thinking that there was already a huge list of things her uncle should probably have told her about. But he didn't get a chance because just then then the door opened, and the most extraordinary-looking woman stepped into the kitchen.

Having been prepared for a lady cyclops with one massive eye, Alice let out a small gasp of astonishment when she found herself looking at a tall woman with smooth skin, wearing a long, white gown, a tartan turban and mirrored sunglasses.

Magnus bounded over from the other side of the kitchen. 'Medusa, it's always a pleasure to see you.'

Medusa stepped towards him and held out an elegant hand. 'Magnus! Such a shame we meet again under such serious circumstances.'

'Do you know each other?' asked Alice.

Medusa nodded. 'Of course. I am the Head of Staff, as well as one of Magnus's clients.' She turned to face Alice, who found herself staring at her own reflection in Medusa's sunglasses.

'This is my niece, Alice,' said Magnus. 'She's sort of doing work experience with me this week.'

'Which sounds so much nicer than babysitting, does it not, Alice?' Medusa said with a smile.

Alice nodded. She'd just been thinking exactly that.

'It is a pleasure to make your acquaintance, Alice,' continued Medusa, bowing her head ever so slightly, 'albeit under such testing circumstances.'

Alice tried to smile encouragingly – this poor

woman had lost her husband, after all – but she couldn't help being a bit distracted by the turban. It seemed to be pulsating.

'I see you are fascinated by my headdress.'

'Oh, well . . . it's . . . it's . . . such a pretty tartan.' Alice felt herself go bright red.

Medusa smiled. 'Thank you. Now, I understand I am to serve you some food.' She lifted the pan lid, shrouding her head in a cloud of steam. 'This is not fit for a swine's supper,' she said, emerging from the pongy fug. 'My husband baked this yesterday,' said Medusa, taking a delicious-smelling loaf out of the bread bin. 'It will nourish, whereas Mrs Stuart's soup will most likely poison us.'

Whilst Medusa busied herself slicing the bread and some cheese, Alice jumped at the chance to consult the *OMG*. She checked the index for Medusa, but it said: *See 'Gorgon'*. When she finally found the right

page, she shuddered at the picture of a woman with snakes for hair.

GORGON		
CATEGORY:		**6**
AVERAGE LIFE SPAN:		**2,500 YEARS +**
HUMAN INTEGRATION:		**HIGHLY INADVISABLE**
SKILLS: PETRIFYING PEOPLE WITH THEIR EYES AND TURNING THEM TO STONE; TELEPATHY; STRONG PERSUASIVE POWERS		
RESTRICTIONS: GORGONS MUST KEEP THEIR EYES AND SNAKES COVERED AT ALL TIMES		
DANGER RATING:		**EXTREME**

A shiver ran down Alice's back like a melting ice cube. So that's what was wriggling under the turban – snakes. She'd be having words with her uncle about this! He must have known about Medusa's snakes. And as if that wasn't terrifying enough, a gorgon could look at you and turn you to stone. Stone dead.

7. MOONLIGHTING

A few minutes later, Medusa returned to the table with a plate of sandwiches.

The beautiful monster folded her hands in her lap. She had the kind of long, elegant fingers that Alice's music teacher said were made for playing the piano – unlike her own, which, as Miss Sharpe had pointed out on more than one occasion, were good only for the triangle.

Alice took a sandwich and smiled at Medusa, hoping she didn't look as terrified as she felt. It wasn't easy, because the more Alice looked at the turban, the more she noticed movement inside it.

A wriggling and writhing, slipping and sliding sort of movement. She half expected something to come slithering out.

SNAKES! WHY DID IT HAVE TO BE SNAKES?

Alice quickly took a bite of sandwich to distract herself. The bread was the tastiest she'd ever eaten.

'Can you think of why Polyphemus might have left?' asked Magnus, fingers poised over his tablet, ready to take notes.

'My husband had not been his usual happy self since receiving a letter from the Ministry of Monsters,' said Medusa, shaking her head. 'But even so, he knows he cannot leave the castle.'

'May I see this letter?' asked Magnus.

Medusa reached into her robe and handed him an envelope. Magnus read the contents with an increasingly shocked face. He pushed it over the table to Alice, who picked it up and read:

Ministry for Monsters

Dear Mr Polyphemus,

In accordance with Directive 462b of the Monster Integration Act, section 74, subsection 18, you are hereby ordered to attend a MFWA (Monster Fitness to Work Assessment). This will include hearing and sight tests. Failure to pass the assessment will result in immediate termination of employment. Please contact the ministry within two weeks to comply with this order.

Have a pleasant day,

Gideon Dragstorm,
Minister for Monsters

Alice was no expert, but she could recognise a threat when she saw one. There was no way a blind cyclops could pass a sight test. There was no way he could have read the letter in the first place! 'Your husband must have been very upset,' she said sympathetically.

'He was,' said Medusa, sighing. 'But he intended to continue working here anyway, for free if necessary.'

'So,' said Magnus, 'you don't think he left the castle to attend this ridiculous assessment?'

'No.' Medusa folded the letter. 'He knows the limits placed on Category Five monsters.'

'Let me get this right,' said Alice. 'The ministry wanted him to take a test he couldn't possibly pass?'

'Yes,' said Magnus.

'And he'd have been breaking monster law if he'd tried to take it?'

Medusa nodded.

Alice looked at Magnus. 'What's going on?'

Magnus shook his head. 'Not sure. It's like a witch-hunt. Or rather, a cyclops-hunt.'

Medusa wiped a tear from her cheek. 'I fear Polyphemus is in grave danger,' she said quietly. 'Please help me find him.'

'I'm sorry he's missing,' said Alice, thinking she ought to be out in the cold looking for him.

'There is a small search party from the castle already out there,' said Medusa, leaving Alice with the odd sensation that she had read her mind.

Alice smiled at the gorgon, then took another bite of her sandwich. She'd just swallowed a mouthful when a shiver rippled through her, right down to her toes, which was weird because it was warm and toasty in the kitchen. *Maybe it's from being so close to those snakes*, thought Alice. But when she looked at her uncle, Alice noticed that he had felt it too.

Magnus was gripping the table as if it was about to run away. Every single hair on him was standing on end, making him look like a ginger, human-sized toilet brush.

Medusa began clearing the table. 'It's going to be clear tonight,' she said. 'With the full moon there will be plenty of light to keep searching for Polyphemus.'

'Oh crikey,' said Magnus. He began frantically emptying the contents of his pockets. Coins, tissues, pen tops and lottery tickets quickly littered the table in front of him.

'What's the matter?' asked Alice.

'You haven't seen a little case anywhere have you, Alice? A green one, like a glasses case, only smaller? With a small bottle inside?'

'No. Is it in the car?'

Magnus looked at Alice. His eyes darted wildly around in their sockets, not fixing on anything.

And they were bloodshot, as if he'd been having a sneezing fit.

'Do you want me to check the car, Uncle Magnus?'

'Yes, maybe. I don't know. I can't have left it anywhere, not today. Oh dear! Oh no!'

Magnus's eyes bulged like red-stained eggs. Then he whimpered and began panting, tongue hanging out, like a puppy that had run about too much in the sun.

Alice rushed over and grabbed her uncle's hand. 'What's the matter?'

Magnus growled weakly. She leaned in closer to hear what he was trying to say.

'Call . . . office . . . anti . . . dote.'

'What?'

Magnus stopped trying to talk, panting instead. Then he let out a low and menacing snarl. The terrible sort of snarl a zombie dog would make whilst making up its mind who to rip to pieces first.

Alice instinctively took a step back, but kept her eyes fixed firmly on her uncle, whose bloodshot eyes were now locked on to her. He tried to say something, but the words turned into a sort of barking noise. Then Magnus pushed back his chair and lurched out of the kitchen, slamming the door behind him so hard that dozens of teapots and cups crashed down from the shelves.

Alice was still staring at the door when Medusa broke the silence.

'Well, that was unexpected,' she said.

'Och, what a carry-on!' said Mrs Stuart, popping back in through the wall. 'I have been grievously terrorised by some beast.' The housekeeper's neat bun had fallen out and her cardigan was hanging off her shoulders.

'Where did it go, Mrs Stuart?' asked Medusa.

The housekeeper pursed her lips until they resembled dried-out maggots. 'It went straight through me, then out the back door,' she said.

"ARRROOOOOOOO!"

A howl echoed from somewhere outside. For the first time ever, Alice understood what 'spine-chilling' really meant. She ran to the window. Even though it had grown dark, the courtyard was bathed in bright, white moonlight. A fountain in the centre sparkled like a firework in the moon's glow.

Medusa took Alice's hand. 'What exactly did your uncle say?'

'I think he said something about an antidote.'

Medusa looked at Mrs Stuart. Then they both looked at Alice.

A second head-piercing howl reverberated

through the castle. With her ears still ringing, Alice took a deep breath.

'Was that my uncle?' she asked them.

Medusa nodded.

'What's wrong with him?'

'It would appear,' said Medusa slowly, 'that Magnus is a werewolf.'

'Aye,' said Mrs Stuart, glaring at Alice with dark eyes. 'And he's loose in the castle grounds.'

8. THE GIRL WHO CRIED WOLF

Alice allowed herself to be led through a door, up a narrow spiral staircase and into a room where she was directed to an armchair.

'This is Their Majesties' private sitting room,' said Medusa. 'We will be safe here.'

Alice just sat there, blinking in the flickering light.

Uncle Magnus!

A werewolf!

She didn't need to look this one up in the guidebook: werewolves bit; they maimed; they killed. She jumped up and dashed to a window, but the moon must have vanished behind a cloud. All she could see was her own terrified face staring back.

'Please, you must sit. You have suffered a shock.' Medusa took Alice's arm and led her back to the armchair.

'But w . . . what if he's out there,' stammered Alice, 'doing bad things?'

'Here, girl, drink this.' Mrs Stuart handed her a cup of tea which clattered in the saucer as Alice took it.

'Thank you,' was all Alice could manage to say. She took a few sips, then reached out to place the cup and saucer on a side table, but missed. The china smashed as it hit the floor and Alice burst into tears. Mrs Stuart tutted and began picking up the pieces whilst Medusa handed Alice a box of tissues.

'Do not worry,' she said kindly, 'it is perfectly normal to cry.'

Alice wiped her eyes, but the tears kept on coming.

She must have got through half the box before she could speak.

'I . . . I don't understand,' she choked out.

'Your uncle simply neglected to take his werewolf antidote,' said Medusa calmly. 'It is now our job to make sure no one comes to any harm.'

'Shouldn't we call someone? The police or the Ministry of, you know, Monsters?'

'Under no circumstances,' snapped Mrs Stuart. 'The minister must not hear about it. No, this little matter will be dealt with amongst ourselves. Like the last time.'

Last time? Alice must have looked confused, because Medusa explained, 'We had a similar issue some years ago. One of the younger royals. Forgot his antidote, just like your uncle. Luckily he tripped over a statue in the rose garden and broke a leg before he could go on a proper rampage.'

'There's a werewolf in the royal family?' sniffed Alice.

'There are werewolves in many families, Alice,' said Medusa.

'Often more than one,' Mrs Stuart said as she bustled out with the broken cup.

Alice looked towards the window nervously. 'But they're dangerous, aren't they?'

'Left to their own devices, yes,' said Medusa. 'But this will not be the case with Magnus.'

Alice was about to say that he might be devouring someone right now, when loud shouting began outside. It sounded like a small army was rushing by. She raced over to the window. Beams of light cut through the darkness, criss-crossing the sky.

Then she heard it. A long, high-pitched and utterly terrifying howl slicing through the night, silencing the shouts and yells. The shouting started up again, but now it was more urgent. 'Over there!' someone screamed.

The beams of light immediately began to converge, sweeping closer together to form a spotlight on the gravel driveway, where something was hunched over. It suddenly lifted its head, opened its jaws lined with saw-sharp teeth, and howled. The noise pierced the night sky and seemed to make even the moon itself vibrate. The creature sprang to its clawed paws, its red, bristly hair gleaming under the spotlights, and then it leaped across the gravel. A split second later, a ball of flames burst over the creature, sending it crashing to the ground. Yelping, it rolled around to put out its blazing fur.

'Uncle Magnus!' cried Alice. And then she fainted.

'Caught you just in time,' said Medusa, holding Alice from behind. She led her back to the armchair. 'Now, sit and take some deep breaths.'

Alice did her best, but her chest felt like she'd just done twenty circuits of the playing field whilst giving a hippopotamus a piggyback.

She sat, shaking, until Mrs Stuart reappeared.

'You'll be pleased to hear that your uncle has survived,' said the housekeeper.

Alice gulped. 'He's not dead?'

Mrs Stuart shook her head. 'No. Injured, but not dead. He has some badly singed fur and is unable to walk at present.'

'What was that fireball thing?' asked Alice.

'The castle phoenix,' said Mrs Stuart. 'It was released not a moment too soon.'

Alice spun round to face Medusa. 'I have to see him. Please!' she begged.

'He'll be cared for tonight. You may see him in the morning,' said Medusa. 'When he's himself again.'

Alice sniffed. She hadn't thought about that possibility. Just because he'd been hurt, didn't mean her uncle wasn't still in full fur, teeth and claws werewolf mode.

'The best thing you can do now is to get some sleep,' said Medusa. 'Mrs Stuart will call Jobs4Monsters to let them know what has happened.'

The housekeeper thrust her long nose into the air. 'If I must.'

'And she will also find you a room to sleep in,' said Medusa.

Mrs Stuart's nose rose even higher. 'Every room is prepared for Their Majesties' guests this weekend.'

'*Every* room?'

'Aye, save the Blue Tartan suite.'

'Well, that will have to do.' Medusa looked at

Alice and smiled gently. 'It's somewhat basic,' she explained, 'and has no electricity.'

The gorgon whistled, and a ball of what Alice had thought was candlelight floated down from the ceiling. It hovered in front of Alice, humming gently.

'This is Glister, a sprite,' said Medusa. 'Their Majesties like to do their bit to save energy and these creatures are the ultimate in renewable power. Glister will stay with you tonight should you prefer not to sleep in darkness.'

Alice squinted into the flickering light. She could just make out a tiny creature with flittering wings. Listening carefully, she realised it wasn't humming, but singing. The sprite nudged Alice's hand, which she opened to allow it to land in her palm. It buzzed and tickled, spreading a warm glow right through her.

'This way,' barked Mrs Stuart, leading Alice out of the sitting room and up another staircase. She pushed open a massive wooden door, sending a musty blast of freezing air rushing past Alice's face. The housekeeper gave her a gentle push into the room. 'Is there anything you need?' she asked.

Alice shook her head and mumbled 'no', as the door slammed in her face.

That wasn't true.

What she needed right now was for her uncle not to be lying unconscious outside with singed werewolf hair all over his body!

9. STABLE CONDITION

Despite everything that had happened, Alice slept soundly. Glister had switched to a dim glow and hummed a soothing tune that made her so relaxed, she drifted off. When she woke up, it took a few moments to work out where she was. Then everything came flooding back to her: the castle, Medusa, her uncle transforming into a werewolf.

The phoenix firebomb.

A sharp rap on the door exploded the image of Magnus smouldering on the ground.

'Porridge,' announced Mrs Stuart, barging in and dumping a tray on top of the bed. 'Eat.' She threw open the curtains. 'Royal sitting room. Fifteen minutes,' she said, before striding out and slamming the door.

Alice sniffed the grey porridge, detecting a cabbagey pong. She forced down a couple of mouthfuls then, with Glister shimmering in front of her, went in search of a bathroom.

A quarter of an hour later, she walked into the sitting room.

'Good morning, Alice,' said Medusa, who was arranging papers at a desk. 'I have just spoken to the royal monstician. Magnus is well enough to receive visitors.' She got up and handed Alice a tablet. 'Your uncle left this in the kitchen. We shall go to the stables and you can return it to him.'

Alice slipped the tablet into her satchel and followed Medusa down the stairs, wondering what a monstician was and why her uncle was in a stable.

'The guest rooms are all ready to receive our royal guests,' said Medusa, her robes billowing behind her and her turban teetering from side to side with every step. 'In any case, Mrs Stuart does not wish your uncle to shed his werewolf hair in one of her freshly made beds. Does that answer your question?'

'I didn't ask one,' said Alice.

'And to answer your other question,' said Medusa, still walking at top speed, 'a monstician is a doctor for monsters.'

Alice's mind swirled with all the weird things that were happening to her. *Is anything ever going to be normal again?* she thought.

'There is no such thing as normal,' said Medusa. 'Surely you have discovered this by now?'

Alice scurried to keep up with Medusa. 'How are you doing that? Reading my mind.'

Medusa paused mid-stride and turned to face her.

'I apologise,' she said. 'It must seem rather odd.'

'Yes, it does,' said Alice. 'I mean, it's a bit of a superpower and everything.'

'We shall talk and walk,' Medusa said, marching off again. 'Mind-reading is just one of the many skills I possess, although it does not work with everyone. Does it bother you?'

Did it? Alice wasn't sure. She'd love to have a superpower. It would make breaktime at school so much more interesting! 'No, it's OK.' She glanced at Medusa's turban again. 'What am I thinking now?'

Medusa laughed. 'You wish to know if it is difficult living with my snakes.'

'And is it?' asked Alice.

'Having a serpentine scalp was not always easy,' said Medusa. 'For many years I hid away, in complete solitude.'

Alice had endured plenty of name-calling for her

ginger hair over the years, but at least she had her friends. It sounded like Medusa had had no friends at all.

'You are right, Alice. It was not easy being friendless and alone.'

'I bet,' said Alice.

'Alas,' continued Medusa, 'being alone was nothing compared to discovering my other power.'

'You mean the whole turning-people-into-stone thing?' Alice asked.

'Yes. It was a shock to discover that I could petrify any living soul with a mere glance. After a few unfortunate accidents, I ran away and hid in dark caves with trolls and minotaurs and dragons. All of us outcasts.' Medusa paused and sighed. 'Life was hard back then. Nowadays, of course, monsters may earn an honest living. My sweet husband and I work here, for example. And trolls do rather well running the internet from their caves.'

So the trolls on the internet actually ARE trolls!
thought Alice.

'Nobody must ever know these things,' said
Medusa, with a warning tone to her voice. She
cleared her throat. 'When I met Polyphemus, it was
love at first sight – at least, it was for me. With him,
I could finally be myself. I could look him straight in
the eye and he would remain flesh and blood. And
my snakes would never scare him. To Polyphemus, I
am beautiful – a goddess. He tells me this each day,
and yet he has never seen my face.'

'You *are* beautiful,' said Alice.

'Thank you,' said the gorgon. 'That's very kind.'
She tapped the side of her sunglasses. 'I hate these
ugly things,' she said, 'but they allow me to live my
life.'

'I think they're cool,' Alice said. 'They suit you.'

'Thank you again,' said Medusa. 'And I appreciate your other kind thought.'

'Which one?' asked Alice.

'That you wish to help me find my husband.'

'Of course, I want to help,' Alice said. 'You think he's in danger, don't you?'

'You can read my mind too?'

'No,' said Alice, 'but I'm right, aren't I?'

Medusa nodded. 'Yes. I believe he is in terrible danger.'

They were still some distance from the stables when the smell hit Alice.

'Yuk! What's that?' Alice exclaimed.

'What is what?' Medusa looked around.

'That smell,' said Alice, holding her nose. 'It's terrible.'

Medusa sniffed. 'I detect nothing. My snakes have a far superior sense of smell, but they are sleeping at present.'

Another putrid whiff of manure and way-past-its-best chicken shot up Alice's nose, mixed with the unmistakable stench of a butcher's shop – all raw meat and blood.

'You really can't smell it?'

Medusa shrugged.

'Doesn't matter,' said Alice. 'I must have imagined it.'

A few minutes later, they reached the stables. Alice rushed in and gave her uncle a hug.

'Oh dear,' he said, 'I must look awful.'

Straw stuck out of his hair, a bandage was wrapped around one leg, and clumps of burnt ginger hair stuck to his blanket.

'You've looked better,' agreed Alice. 'But on the plus side, at least you're human again!'

Magnus smiled a not-very-convincing smile. 'It only lasts whilst the moon's up,' he said.

'You must be cold though,' said Alice, 'without your clothes.'

'They're finding me some new ones,' said Magnus, pulling the blanket up to his neck. 'I'm afraid I ripped mine off last night.' He winced as he shifted position in the straw.

'Does it hurt?'

Magnus nodded. 'Mainly where the flames got through to my skin. Look, about last night . . . I mean . . . you know . . .'

'It's OK.' Alice sat down in the straw next to her uncle. 'I wish you'd told me. I might have been able to help.'

'I doubt it,' said Magnus. 'Once the mutation is triggered by the moon and released into the bloodstream, it's already too late.' He leaned over and gave Alice a hug, before collapsing back into his nest of straw. An odour like damp dogs hung over him, which Alice decided not to mention. 'It must have been a horrible shock, Alice. I'm sorry.'

'It was,' said Alice. 'Everything happened so quickly. One minute you were chatting away, the next you went all weird.'

'I can't believe I lost my antidote. I've never done that before.' He groaned. 'I'll have to turn myself in, you know.'

'Who to?' asked Alice.

'The ministry,' said Magnus. 'I broke so many monster laws last night, I'll be lucky to even get a trial. The Monster Integration Act forbids werewolves to transform. And with Dragstorm's crackdown . . .'

'The minister does not need to know,' said Medusa, who was standing by the stable's gate.

Magnus shifted uncomfortably. 'Maybe not immediately,' he said, as Alice bundled some straw into a sort of pillow for him, 'but news will get out. It always does.' He lay back down and closed his eyes. He looked totally exhausted; his face was pale and there were dark smudges all around his eyes, which suddenly popped open again. 'Oh no! I completely forgot about Polyphemus. Has he been found?'

'He's still missing,' said Alice. 'The search party ended up looking for you instead last night.'

Magnus buried his head in his arms. 'I'm so sorry, Medusa.'

The gorgon sighed. 'It doesn't matter. I believe my husband was already far away from this place.'

Alice turned to Medusa. 'You think he's been taken, don't you?'

'Yes,' she said sadly. 'Although by whom, I cannot say.'

Alice really wanted to help but with so few clues it was next to impossible.

'When did he disappear?' she asked.

'Before lunch,' replied Medusa. 'He usually helps with deliveries in the morning.'

'And that's what he was doing yesterday?' asked Magnus.

Medusa shrugged. 'I was elsewhere in the castle. You would need to ask Mrs Stuart.'

'Now's your chance,' said Magnus. 'She's just outside.'

Alice stared at her uncle. 'How do you know?'

'I can hear her talking to someone.'

Alice couldn't hear anything. 'But that's impossible.'

'Not really,' said Magnus. 'Most werewolves have

one permanently heightened sense. Hearing is mine.'

Medusa walked out and reappeared seconds later with the housekeeper.

'This had better be important,' barked Mrs Stuart. 'I've a castle full of rooms to clean and now they tell me the Danish royals are bringing their centaur! The last time he was here, he demanded a mattress *and* straw, and since you're taking up this stall, I have to find another one.'

'It is important,' said Magnus. 'We need to know what Polyphemus was doing yesterday morning.'

Mrs Stuart huffed with impatience. 'Dealing with deliveries, I suppose. I'd been up since five, so was trying to take my morning nap.'

'Trying?' asked Alice.

'Yes,' snapped Mrs Stuart. 'You try sleeping with a delivery truck scraping over every speed bump on its way out.'

'It woke you up as it was leaving, but not as it arrived?' asked Alice.

'That's what I said.'

Alice frowned. 'Isn't that a bit odd? You'd think a delivery truck would be lighter on its way out.'

Magnus leaned forward, yelping in pain. 'Ouch! It would be, unless it wasn't delivering anything . . . but taking it away! You're a genius, Alice!'

10. MONSTER HUNTERS

Mrs Stuart narrowed her eyes as if she was processing the information. 'You think the cyclops was in the truck?'

Alice turned to her. 'Why not?'

Pursing her lips until the colour drained out of them, Mrs Stuart was silent for a moment. 'The vehicle was certainly large enough,' she said finally.

'You saw it!' cried Alice.

'Aye, of course. It was a big white van.'

'Anything else?' asked Magnus.

The housekeeper turned her gaze on him, her upper lip curled in disdain like a Turkish slipper.

'Such as?'

'Such as a registration number.'

Mrs Stuart sniffed and produced a small, leather-bound notebook from her cardigan pocket. 'Naturally. I intended to report the driver for inconsiderate driving.' She ripped the page out and handed it to Alice. 'You've saved me that job at least.' She gave them one final glare then faded away.

Medusa took the registration number from Alice. 'I will get this traced.'

'You can do that?' asked Alice.

Medusa flashed her film star smile. 'I can do many things.'

As they waited, Alice set about trying to make Magnus more comfortable. He'd just got himself settled when a pterodactyl-like squawk filled the stables. Alice instinctively ducked, but nothing appeared. Instead, a scratching noise vibrated

through the stable partition, followed by the sound of something wet and heavy being slapped around like a slab of meat on a butcher's block.

She suddenly felt something dripping down her cheek. 'Ughh! Blood!' Alice plunged a hand into her bag and whipped out her umbrella.

'Excellent,' laughed Magnus. 'Just like a scout – ready for anything.'

Alice held the umbrella over them both. 'Mum

made me bring it. She said it rained a lot in Scotland, but I didn't think she meant it would be raining blood.'

The creature squawked again.

'That's not a horse, is it?'

Magnus yawned. 'No, and whatever it is, it's been making a racket all morning. Every time I drop off, it either squawks, screeches or farts.'

Alice left Magnus under the umbrella and walked over to the partition, jumping to try and see over the top.

'Careful!' warned Magnus, as another flesh-ripping sound reverberated through the stables. 'I'm not sure it's friendly.'

'Eeww!' A spongy piece of meat, oozing blood, landed on the floor by Alice's foot. She flung the morsel back over the partition, setting off a crazed scurrying and more loud squawking. Then, whatever it was quietened down and began snoring, interspersed with long, bubbling burps.

This is my chance to get a look! Alice crept towards the gate, but she stopped when her satchel started vibrating noisily. The creature next door snuffled awake and began scratching again.

'You're ringing,' said Magnus.

'I can't be,' said Alice. 'I haven't got a phone. Not allowed one.'

Magnus pointed to her satchel. 'Well, something in there's ringing.'

Alice reached in and pulled out Magnus's tablet. 'I forgot I had this,' she said, handing it to her uncle. He tapped the screen and Miss Pinky's face sprang into view.

'Hi guys! It's me!' she shouted. 'Can you hear me?'

'Yes, Miss Pinky,' said Magnus. 'Loud and very clear.'

'Magnus! It's you! And you're not all hairy and scary. Epic mistake yesterday. And at the castle. Classy!' She waved a small green case in front of the camera. 'Look what I found!'

'My antidote!' cried Magnus.

'It was under the sofa,' said Miss Pinky, her smile stretching the whole width of the screen. 'You must have lost it when the banshee went bonkers yesterday.'

Magnus sighed and collapsed back into his straw bed. 'I can't believe I was so careless,' he said.

'Don't worry about that,' said Miss Pinky. 'I have some major gossip. My mermate Pearl's been messaging all morning about the date she went on yesterday with this super cool merman. He calls himself Neptune, but I think his real name's Nevil, or something . . . anyway, she was on this date—'

'Miss Pinky,' interrupted Magnus, 'unless this is

important, we haven't got time for gossip.'

On the screen, Miss Pinky's eyes narrowed. 'Just because you went all werewolf last night, doesn't mean you should bite my head off now,' she snapped. 'And yes, it is important.'

'Go on, Miss Pinky,' said Alice, wanting to hear more about the mermaids. 'We're listening. Aren't we, Uncle Magnus?' She elbowed him.

'Yes, yes, all right. Go on.'

'Thank you,' said Miss Pinky. 'So, as I was saying, Pearl and Neptune were hanging out on this island off the coast of Edinburgh last night. Humans haven't used it for years, so it's a perfect spot to chill. But then they got interrupted.'

'By what?' asked Alice.

'Well,' said Miss Pinky, 'Pearl called it a "right kerfuffle". She said a boat arrived and something really big was hauled ashore. It was the middle of the night, so she didn't get a good look, but she reckons it was as big as three grown mermen.'

Alice felt a tingle begin to work its way up her spine.

'But here's the really interesting part,' said Miss Pinky, whose eyes were sparkling with excitement. 'Pearl says she heard someone shout, "move it, one-eye!"'

Magnus and Alice stared at each other, then back at the screen.

'Are you sure?' asked Magnus.

Miss Pinky nodded vigorously, making her whiskers quiver. 'That's what she said. It can't be a coincidence. It must have been Polyphemus.'

'I agree,' said Magnus.

'Right, I'll email the details,' said Miss Pinky. 'Got to run. I placed an order with Doogie and he's just pinged me to say it's ready. Bye!'

As soon as the email arrived, Alice and Magnus looked up the exact location on a map. As Miss Pinky had said, it was a small island, just to the west of the city.

'Ah,' said Medusa, sweeping back in. 'I see you have a map on your device. Will you be so kind as to input these co-ordinates?' She handed Alice a piece of paper. 'The last sighting of the delivery van on CCTV,' she explained. 'I pulled a few strings with a witch I know at the Department of Transport.'

Magnus tapped the numbers into the tablet. 'Bingo!' he cried. 'It's almost exactly where Pearl was.'

'That's definitely not a coincidence,' said Alice, staring at the map. She zoomed in on the rocky speck in the middle of the water. 'There's a building on the island,' she said, showing Magnus and Medusa, 'and it looks big enough to hide a cyclops.'

Medusa smiled and placed her hand on Alice's shoulder. 'I'm thinking exactly what you're thinking,' she said.

Alice raised her eyebrows. 'Go on then,' she said, 'what am I thinking?'

'That we should investigate this island right away,' replied Medusa.

'No!' said Magnus, shaking his head. 'I promised Alice's mum I'd look after her.'

Alice and Medusa stared at him.

'OK,' he said, 'so I kind of failed last night.'

Alice laughed. 'Kind of?'

Magnus pulled the blanket up again and shivered. 'All I'm saying is, it might be dangerous.'

'It might,' agreed Alice.

'Plus,' said Magnus, 'you've already had to deal with' – he dropped his voice to a whisper – 'snakes.'

'Exactly,' Alice whispered back, 'so what are the

chances of having to face any more of my phobias?'
She turned to Medusa. 'I'd like to come, though I'm
not sure how helpful I'll be.'

Medusa was silent for a moment. Then she took
Alice's hand and spoke. 'You are intelligent and
resourceful, and whilst you may not be fearless, you
are determined to help me find my husband. Bravery
in the face of fear is a far more useful weapon than
any other.'

Alice was amazed. 'You got all that from reading
my mind?'

'She didn't need to,' said Magnus. 'It's who you
are and I'm very proud that you're my niece.'

Alice rushed over to give him a hug. 'Thank you,'
she said. 'I promise to be careful.'

Magnus nodded. 'I know you will be. But I think
it might be sensible to have Miss Pinky meet you
there. If things look too dangerous, she can take you

back to Edinburgh. How does that sound, Medusa?'

Alice could have sworn she heard hissing from inside Medusa's turban.

'I can assure you that Alice will be quite safe with me,' said the gorgon.

'Yes, I'm sure she will,' said Magnus, 'but just in case.'

Medusa sniffed and reached for the tablet. 'Very well,' she said, looking at the map. She pointed to a position on the mainland, a short distance from the island. 'Tell Miss Pinky to meet us here. It is an abandoned harbour where our arrival will not be seen.' With that, she glided out of the stall and into the one next door, setting the creature off on another round of clawing and squawking.

Alice tried to ignore the commotion. Had she really just agreed to dash across the country into who-knew-what danger, leaving her injured uncle lying in a stable?

'Maybe I should stay with you,' she said to Magnus. 'What if the ministry comes and tries to take you away?'

'Finding Polyphemus is the most important thing right now,' replied Magnus. 'We can worry about me later. And anyway, it sounds like Medusa's ready for you.'

Alice looked out of the stall as Medusa struggled past, dragging a creature out on a thick rope. It had kicked up a cloud of straw and dust, but Alice caught a glimpse of massive claws, a sharp beak and silvery feathers.

'Oh no!' wailed Alice. 'Does that thing fly?'

Magnus pulled Alice down and gave her a goodbye hug. 'There's probably no seatbelts, so don't forget to hold on tight!'

11. YOUR NEAREST EXIT MAY BE BEHIND YOU

Alice stepped out into the stable yard and immediately pancaked herself against the wall to avoid being swept off her feet by the creature's vast, silver-grey wings.

'He's a touch frisky to start with,' shouted Medusa, 'but he soon calms down.'

'How soon?' Alice shouted back, blinking as the tips of its wings brushed her face. Her heart felt like it was lodged in her mouth as images of chunks of meat and buckets of blood raced through her head. She didn't dare move until the animal had settled itself on the cobbles and folded its wings over its smooth, golden back.

'Alice, come and meet Gordon.' Medusa rolled up his leash. 'Our transport south.'

Alice edged around the yard until she was face-to-face – or, more accurately, face-to-beak – with the creature. Piercing yellow eyes stared out from a massive eagle's face.

'He's a griffin, isn't he?' said Alice, remembering something she'd seen in the *OMG*. 'Half lion, half eagle?'

'Yes,' said Medusa, 'a royal griffin.'

Gordon stared at Alice, his inky black pupils reflecting tiny versions of herself. He blinked and squawked gently.

'He likes you,' said Medusa.

'That's good,' said Alice, ignoring the farty stink wafting from the griffin's hindquarters and taking a closer look at him. His rear paws were the size

of cannonballs. His hooked talons at the front appeared capable of shredding an elephant into mince in seconds.

'Watch his beak,' warned Medusa. 'It's supremely sharp.'

Alice ducked to avoid contact with Gordon as he waved his head from side to side, flexing his long neck and squawking. Medusa produced a bunch of mint leaves from her robe and fed them to the griffin, who eagerly gulped them down. 'For his appalling halitosis,' she whispered. 'Now, it is time to take to the skies.'

Alice's heart rate instantly increased to that of a hamster stuck in a wheel whilst rolling down a mountain.

FLYING! WHY DID IT HAVE TO BE FLYING?

'You are scared,' said Medusa. 'Am I correct?'

'Yep,' said Alice, feeling an uncomfortable tightness cinch her chest like a belt, 'flying's my number one phobia.'

'And snakes are your second, I think,' said Medusa, a hint of a smile on her lips.

Alice shrugged. There was no hiding anything from the gorgon.

'But I sense you are excited as well as terrified,' said Medusa, 'and that your desire for adventure is greater than your fear – as it is with all the best heroes.' She held out a hand to Alice. 'Come, it is time to fly.'

Alice stepped up on to Gordon's cannonball paw, reached for a handful of his silvery feathers and heaved herself into position on his back. Beneath his lion's body, she could feel the creature's heart thudding. Then, as Medusa climbed up behind her, his enormous wings began beating. Alice grabbed some more of the griffin's feathers and she felt Medusa's arms wrap around her waist.

'Do not be scared,' whispered the gorgon. 'We will come to no harm.'

Then, as Gordon's wings began to flap more quickly and they were lifted high into the air, Alice dared to look down. The castle had become a tiny dot in an ocean of trees, whilst rivers and lakes twinkled in the sunshine like diamonds sprinkled across the landscape.

Suddenly, they were thrust forward as Gordon dipped towards the ground.

Alice screamed.

'Do not worry,' shouted Medusa over the rush of air. 'He is looking for a warm current.'

Sure enough, they levelled out seconds later and began flitting through the clouds. This pattern repeated itself, Alice's stomach going into high-speed spin-dry as they nosedived, then settling as they rose again. This wasn't what she imagined flying would feel like. This was . . .

'Amazing, isn't it?' yelled Medusa.

Alice didn't bother shouting back. Medusa would know what she was thinking anyway: Yes! Flying on a griffin *was* amazing!

In what seemed like no time, Medusa let go of Alice to point through a hole in the clouds.

'We're there,' she said,
as Gordon tipped his wings
and headed for the gap in the swirling clouds.
Alice caught a glimpse of a bridge, white-capped
waves crashing on to its legs, and beyond it, a rocky
island.

'It's windy,' said Medusa. 'We must brace for
turbulence.'

Seconds later, they began spinning in a sort of
high-velocity, aerial corkscrew. A massive gust sent
them sideways into a dark cloud where they were
pelted with hailstones. Bursting out again,

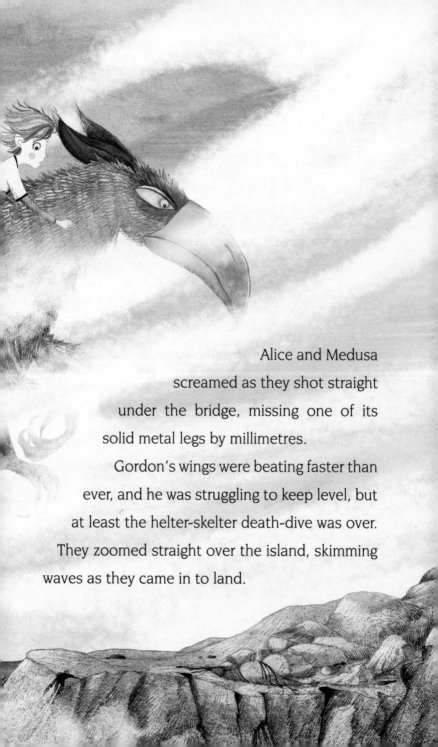

Alice and Medusa
screamed as they shot straight
under the bridge, missing one of its
solid metal legs by millimetres.

Gordon's wings were beating faster than
ever, and he was struggling to keep level, but
at least the helter-skelter death-dive was over.
They zoomed straight over the island, skimming
waves as they came in to land.

'Hold tight!' screamed Medusa.

Landing in a plane was one thing. They had wheels. And seatbelts. And lifejackets. *All of which might be useful right now*, thought Alice, as Gordon approached what looked like a pier, jutting out into the water from the mainland. Lightning flashed around them and a rumble of thunder vibrated in Alice's chest, but somehow the griffin stayed horizontal as they dropped towards the end of the pier.

WHAM!

One of Gordon's paws made contact.
Then the griffin bounced back
into the air.

THWACK!

His wing hit the pier as a gust of
wind buffeted them to one side.

SLAM!

Both paws hit the ground.

SCREEEEECH!

His claws scraped along the pier like fingernails down a chalkboard as they hurtled towards a cluster of stone buildings zooming up in front of them.

'Gordon,' Alice screamed, as she was jolted from side to side, 'slow down!' She clamped her eyes shut and braced for impact.

12. TAXI!

Several claw-grinding, paw-bruising moments later, they screeched to a stop. Alice opened her eyes. They were so close to a wall, she could reach out and touch it. Gordon produced one loud roar-squawk before slumping forward, his great beaked head resting on the stone.

'Wow,' gasped Alice, sliding down from Gordon's back. She wasn't sure if she'd been more terrified than excited, or the other way around. Probably somewhere in between.

'Thank you, most noble steed, for our safe deliverance,' said Medusa, placing a hand on the griffin's side.

Gordon attempted to lift his head but gave up and rested it back on the pier.

'I think he's hurt,' said Alice. 'He looks very uncomfortable.'

Medusa began inspecting him. 'Oh no! This is a catastrophe!' She held up the tip of the griffin's left wing. 'See? It must have snapped during landing. He can't fly like this.' She gently laid the wing back on the ground.

Alice stroked Gordon's head. 'Poor thing,' she whispered, as rain began pouring down. 'He can't stay out here,' she said. 'Not in this weather. What if someone sees him?'

Medusa pointed to an abandoned shed by the old stone buildings. 'We must move him there,' she said, coaxing Gordon to his paws and claws. After making the griffin as comfortable as possible, Alice and Medusa walked back on to the pier. Out in the middle of the water, almost hidden by the curtain of rain pelting down, the island seemed impossible to reach.

'Wowza! I thought you were RIP!' Miss Pinky appeared, running down the pier. She was decked out in a bright purple rain cape, which matched her boots perfectly. 'What an epic landing! I saw the whole thing. Nearly got knocked down as you came in.'

Alice rushed up and gave Miss Pinky a massive – if wet – hug. 'It was terrifying,' she cried. 'Terrifying *and* epic.' Then she remembered what Magnus had said. 'Do I have to go back with you?'

Miss Pinky looked surprised. 'Wasn't that dangerous enough for you?'

'Well, yes, I suppose,' said Alice, 'but I kind of enjoyed it too.'

'You kind of enjoyed nearly dying?'

Alice laughed. 'Not the nearly dying bit, no. But the rest of it was amazing! I never get to do daring stuff like this at home.' She thought about how her mum didn't even let her near Grandad Bertie's tiny little dog, which seemed a bit ridiculous now.

'I'm not sure Magnus would approve,' said Miss Pinky. She turned to Medusa and sniffed. 'You always did like to make an entrance.'

Medusa wiped the rain off her sunglasses and looked Miss Pinky up and down. 'Likewise,' she said.

Alice looked out to the island. *She* might not be going, but Medusa still needed to get there. 'How will you cross the water?' she asked the gorgon.

Medusa shook her head. 'I do not know.'

Miss Pinky began jumping up and down in a puddle, splashing water everywhere. 'I do! I do!' she said excitedly. 'I was on the case as soon as I saw your crash landing.' She rummaged in her cape and pulled out her mobile. 'I got straight on to this new monster taxi app called "Chuber", and your new ride should be here soon, Medusa.'

'Why's it called "Chuber"?' asked Alice.

Miss Pinky laughed. 'Because you might get chewed by your taxi, of course!' She pointed towards the dark, rolling water. 'Any minute now.'

Alice followed Miss Pinky's gaze over the churning sea. The wind was whipping the water up into a stampede of foam-topped waves. Then she picked up a scent amongst the salty, seaweedy spray. Alice couldn't quite place it, but it was there, stuck like glue to the back of her nose. There was a mustiness too, similar to the sweaty, leathery smell of the stable.

'There he is!' squealed Miss Pinky, pointing across the water. 'Here's Kevin.'

Medusa cleared her throat. 'Miss Pinky, would you care to tell us who – or what – Kevin is?'

Miss Pinky beamed a sharp-toothed smile in their direction. 'Kevin? He's a kelpie.'

She began jumping and waving as the sea reared up and rolled towards the pier like a super-charged tidal wave.

Alice stared, transfixed, as the wave turned into a dome of water, rising higher and higher, like a submarine about to break through the surface. She gasped as a huge white horse glided effortlessly from the churning sea, transferring from the water to the pier in a single, elegant leap. It trotted towards them, lifting each leg purposefully, like a dressage horse performing in a riding ring. Its white sides glistened with water droplets. The animal threw back its head, neighed and shook its sparkling silvery mane, showering everyone with water.

Alice wiped her eyes, watching Medusa wring out the loose end of her turban.

'Kevin, you naughty, naughty kelpie,' said Miss Pinky.

The creature standing in front of them didn't look much different to a normal horse. Apart from his huge size. And the fact that water poured from his shimmering mane in a constant flow, coursing down his sides and on to the pier.

'Good morning, friends! And what a morning it is to be out on the water. Magnificent!'

And apart from the fact he could talk.

'What can I do for you?' Kevin's voice was deep and serious-sounding.

It's just right, thought Alice, *for a talking horse*.

'Medusa needs to get out of here and over there,' said Miss Pinky, pointing to the island, 'and pronto.'

Medusa approached the kelpie cautiously. 'Do you promise not to drown me?'

Kevin flared his massive nostrils and snorted, his breath misting up Medusa's sunglasses. 'It is many years since us kelpies did that.'

'Did you used to?' asked Alice, taking a step back.

Kevin lowered his head and nodded. 'Alas, yes.

147

Kelpies were once known to lure people into the water and drown them.'

'I thought you ate them too,' said Miss Pinky.

'We did,' said Kevin. 'Well, apart from the livers.'

Miss Pinky shuddered. 'Don't blame you. Who likes liver?'

'Not me,' said Alice, 'but I'm vegetarian.'

'Are you?' asked Miss Pinky, sounding surprised.

'Yes. My mum won't let me eat meat,' explained Alice. 'She says it used to make me aggressive when I was a toddler.'

Medusa interrupted them. 'We do not have time for small talk,' she said. 'It's time to go.'

Alice stared across the waves at the island. She'd come so far, she kind of wanted to continue on the mission. 'What's that?' she asked, spotting a green blur emerging from the black clouds.

Everyone turned to look where Alice was pointing.

'Oh no!' exclaimed Miss Pinky.

'Impossible!' roared Kevin, stamping the pier.

'Take cover!' screamed Medusa.

The kelpie plunged back into the sea, whilst the others dived behind a pile of old lobster pots, pulling some rotten fishing nets over their heads. Through the stinky netting, Alice could make out a group of small green creatures flying in formation like an aerial display team. They shot past and soared up and away into the sky.

Fixies! said Medusa, untangling the net from her turban.

Alice clambered out, crunching over some dried-out mussel shells. 'What are they?'

'Nasty little things,' said Miss Pinky, pulling fish bones out of her long hair. 'A sort of fairy crossed with a pixie.'

Alice had always thought pixies were sweet

creatures, skipping round toadstools in
the moonlight. 'Aren't pixies friendly?'

Miss Pinky shrieked with laughter.
'Hardly! Naughty little devils. Totally
unreliable. But those things are *fixies* – pure evil.
They were banished to a forest in the Highlands years
ago, and had their wings clipped for bad behaviour.'

Alice winced. 'That doesn't sound very kind.'

Medusa snorted. 'Wing-clipping was too good for
them.' She turned to Alice. 'In the Middle Ages, they
used to steal babies from cradles.'

'For fun?' asked Alice.

'To eat,' said Medusa.

Alice gulped. 'What are they doing here?'

'Surveillance, I should imagine,' said Medusa. 'For
whoever on that island is holding my husband.'

'If someone took the trouble to bring the fixies
back,' said Miss Pinky, 'they *really* don't want anyone

getting over there.'

'We must leave this instant,' said Medusa. 'If the fixies see us, they will attack.'

'I'm not being sent back to Edinburgh, then?' asked Alice.

Medusa shook her head. 'You are safer with me. I promised to protect you, and I shall.'

'What about me? Will you protect me too?' asked Miss Pinky.

'Naturally,' said Medusa. 'We all stick together.'

So, this is actually happening, thought Alice, *I'm going to the island*. As Alice realised this, she also noticed she was holding her breath. She still wasn't sure if it was excitement or terror she was feeling. 'Um, do you think I should be going? I'm only just eleven, after all.'

'Eleven! Big deal! I'm only eight and a half.'

Alice stared at Miss Pinky. 'Seriously?'

'Aye,' said Miss Pinky. 'Splicers mature at an incredible rate. I was potty trained at two months and wiping my own bum at—'

'TMI!' Alice couldn't help laughing.

'If you have both quite finished,' said Medusa, 'I suggest we leave immediately.'

'What if the fixies follow us?' asked Alice.

'Nay, don't worry about that,' said Kevin, who had re-emerged from the water. 'I can kick up enough spray to mask an oil tanker. All aboard!'

'Go on,' said Alice, nudging Miss Pinky. 'You first.'

Miss Pinky remained rooted to the spot, shaking slightly. The colour had drained from her face – even her hair seemed less green.

'I can't,' she whispered. 'I know I'm half mermaid, but right now I'm more cat. Why do you think I wear these wellies? It's not just to hide my paws, you know. I hate getting them wet!'

'I'll go first,' Alice groaned, pushing her way past. She stared up at the kelpie, wondering how exactly she was supposed to get on his back.

'Place your hands on my side,' said Kevin.

Alice's hands touched the kelpie's side and immediately became stuck on something. It felt like a cross between gloopy, uncooked egg whites and not-quite-dry paint. She found that by unsticking one hand at a time she could climb up Kevin's side

– a bit like a gecko climbing a wall.

In no time, she'd reached the top and secured herself by sticking her legs firmly either side of Kevin's back. No wonder kelpies had found it easy to drag people to their watery graves: they stuck to them like stamps on an envelope!

Miss Pinky and Medusa quickly climbed into place behind Alice, then Kevin whinnied, shook his mane majestically from side to side – spraying water everywhere – and stepped gracefully into the waves rolling up the slipway.

As Kevin began to swim, Alice glanced up. The fixies had formed into an arrow and it was pointing straight at them. **'Quick!'** she screamed.

'They're dive-bombing!'

13. SALTWATER PEARL

Kevin kicked his hooves, sending up spray like a massive, turbo-powered jet ski. This, combined with the gigantic waves surging across the sea, meant they were hidden from the fixie squadron. Unfortunately, it also meant their ride was anything but smooth. With every wave came an uncomfortable jolt which sent Alice surging into Kevin's sticky mane, then reeling back into Miss Pinky. She felt like a rag doll strapped on to a bucking bronco.

The further Kevin swam away from the pier, the taller the waves became. But as he changed course towards the island, they began to ride the swells, rather than crash into them.

Alice's stomach lurched as a huge wave pushed them up high. Kevin seemed to be fighting to stay on its crest as his legs frantically kicked under the surface. Suddenly, the kelpie splayed his legs, pond skater-style, and for the briefest moment, they were surfing on the top of the wave!

Then down they plunged.

Alice's scream was lost in the roar of the wind and the crash of water. She braced herself for a bone-breaking splashdown, but instead Kevin skimmed like a pebble skipping across the sea, bouncing over the waves until he finally regained control.

Suddenly Miss Pinky yelped like a cat whose paw had been trodden on. 'Ouch!' she yelled through the gale-force wind gusting all around them. 'Medusa, that hurt!'

'It's not my fault,' Medusa called back.

'They're your snakes!' Miss Pinky shouted.

Alice peeked over her shoulder. *Yikes!* Nothing could have prepared her for the sight of eight grey snakes whipping around Medusa's head, tongues flicking and jaws snapping.

Miss Pinky was dodging left and right, trying to avoid their fangs.

'My snakes were drowning,' yelled Medusa, holding her drenched turban in one hand. 'I had to release them.'

A freezing-cold wave smashed into them, flipping everyone over as if they were riding a banana boat in a tornado. Alice managed to gulp some air before water rushed over her, tugging at her clothes and ripping through her hair. There was nothing she could do but hang on to Kevin and hold her breath.

They couldn't have been underwater for more than a few seconds before they burst through the surface like an empty plastic bottle held under water in the bath.

'Sorry,' gasped Kevin. 'Didn't see that one coming.'

Cold and soaking wet, Alice was too shocked to speak. But Miss Pinky was purring with delight.

'That was epic,' she squealed, her fear of water forgotten. 'My followers will love it! My adrenalin's rushing faster than an Apple Store crowd on product launch day.'

Medusa hissed, 'Sshh! We're approaching the island.'

Kevin paddled under the rocky cliffs which loomed above them, seagulls soaring and swooping all around. 'I'll try and find somewhere to drop you off,' he said.

Alice thought she could hear a voice calling out over the noisy gulls screeching overhead. 'Can you guys hear that?' she asked. 'Listen.'

For a moment, there was just the seabirds squawking, but then there it was again.

'Cooeee! Over here, luvvies!'

Alice scanned the shoreline and suddenly spotted someone waving to them. 'Look! We should head over there.'

'No!' said Medusa, firmly. 'It may be a trap.'

Miss Pinky giggled. 'Ha! That's not a trap. That's my mermaid bestie, Pearl. She's the one who tipped us off about this island. Kevin, can you moor up, or dock or whatever, by that rock she's sitting on?'

Kevin swam up alongside the rock and Alice stared up at the mermaid slowly flapping her blue and green-scaled fish tail. Long, straggly grey hair hung limply over her shoulders and she was wearing a bikini top that seemed to be made out of old plastic funnels. Sniffing, Alice detected a fusty odour a bit like her nana's wardrobe.

159

'All right, loves?' said the mermaid. 'I won't get up. I'm like a fish out of water here, I am!' She waved at Alice. 'I'm Pearl, by the way. You should see your face, dearie!'

Alice closed her mouth and tried to smile as if meeting mermaids was something she did every day.

'Not quite what you expected, love?' said Pearl. 'We can't all be called Ariel and swim around in coconut bikinis, you know.'

'Thanks for the message, Pearl,' said Miss Pinky. 'How's that job we found for you, by the way?'

The old mermaid laughed. 'I can't pretend cleaning barnacles off the underside of nuclear submarines is my dream job, but at my age, you take what you can get.'

Medusa hissed under her breath. 'This is all most interesting,' she said. 'But do you have any information of use to us?'

'Get her!' cackled Pearl. 'All hoity-toity. And I thought I was having a bad hair day! Ha!'

Alice glanced behind her and saw Medusa's snakes swirling around, flicking their tongues at the mermaid.

'All right, all right,' said Pearl. 'Keep your snakes on! Come ashore and I'll tell you what I know.'

Everyone clambered off Kevin's back and up on to the rock, where they stood, dripping, whilst Pearl gabbled on.

'There's been all sorts going on here, I tell you,' she said. 'First off, there was all them boats – night and day they was coming and going. No one's set foot or fin on this island for years and now it's like Ibiza in August! Then, all them slimy little selkies kept creeping out of the water. You know there's trouble when they start showing up.'

'Ugh!' Miss Pinky shuddered. 'I hate selkies. All sad-face eyes and sealskin onesies.'

'What's a selkie?' asked Alice.

'They'll be in the *OMG*,' said Miss Pinky. 'They're half human and half seal.'

'And a whole lot of devious,' said Pearl. 'I wouldn't trust them further than I could throw a fish at them.'

'Anything else?' asked Medusa.

'Yes,' said Pearl. 'My mate Myrtle reckons they've got themselves a kraken hidden away somewhere.'

'A kraken?' cried Medusa. 'Impossible!'

'Eek!' screamed Miss Pinky. 'Let's get out of here!'

'Er, guys,' said Alice. 'What's a kraken?'

Pearl grabbed Alice's hand and pulled her down so their heads were level. The mermaid's eyes seemed to contain all the colours of the ocean. 'A kraken is a deadly sea monster that eats anything it fancies – whales, fishing boats, that sort of thing.'

'Why would there be one of them here?' asked Alice nervously.

'Couldn't tell you,' said Pearl, 'but if Myrtle says she saw one being towed here, then I believe her.' She shivered and shook her head. 'I don't fancy your chances against whatever or whoever is on this island,' she said, 'but if there's anything I can do, you know where to find me.'

'Likewise,' said Kevin solemnly, in his deep voice. 'I shall remain nearby.'

'Thank you,' said Medusa. 'And now we must continue.'

Alice wondered when her luck would run out. She'd just survived a crash-landing, kamikaze fixies, and a near-drowning. It now seemed likely that she was going to be munched by a kraken.

'Do not fear,' said Medusa, beginning to climb up the cliff. 'It probably won't come to that.'

After a knuckle-scraping, knee-bashing climb, Alice reached the top of the rocks. Miss Pinky and Medusa helped her over the ledge and they rested for a minute to catch their breath. Suddenly, Alice noticed a really bad smell in the air. It reminded her of an out-of-date pork chop she'd found in her granny's fridge once.

'Something up here really stinks,' she said.

Medusa's snakes writhed, tasting the air with their forked tongues. Alice kept a wary eye on them in case one of them decided to taste her as well.

'We smell nothing,' said Medusa.

'Well I do,' said Alice, 'and it's not good.'

Miss Pinky gawped at her. 'I didn't know you had super-smellability!'

Alice shrugged. 'It's nothing special.'

'Yeah, right!' Miss Pinky laughed. 'With Magnus's hearing and your smelling, you've got a superhero film franchise. Ha!'

'Shh!' Medusa touched a long finger to her lips. She hoisted up her long robes, still dripping from their sea crossing. 'Whatever it is you smell, Alice, we will face it together.'

They walked up a small hill. As they approached the summit, Medusa's snakes stretched up, acting like a submarine's periscope. 'It's clear,' said Medusa.

From the top of the hill, they could see a group of crumbling buildings built into the rocks.

'It looks like a wartime fortress,' said Medusa. 'Of course! There will be bunkers beneath it.'

'Perfect for hiding monsters,' said Alice.

'Er, guys,' said Miss Pinky, pointing just beyond the fortress. 'Epic problem approaching from the west.'

A group of creatures were staggering up the stony path, arms outstretched and mouths hanging open.

'Gah!' Miss Pinky clamped a hand over her mouth and nose. 'Is that what you were smelling?' she asked, through her fingers.

'Yep,' said Alice, wondering if she might throw up. It was a truly revolting stink.

'Ghouls,' said Medusa, whose snakes had curled in on themselves to hide from the stench.

'Are they in the *OMG*?' asked Alice, reaching inside her satchel.

'I'll save you the bother,' said Miss Pinky, holding her nose. 'Their only skill is eating flesh – preferably fresh.'

Alice gulped. 'So they're dangerous, then?'

'Look at them!' Miss Pinky shrieked. 'Do they seem friendly?'

'Do not panic,' said Medusa, calmly. 'There is an entrance there, see?' Alice followed Medusa's long finger. 'If we run,' Medusa continued, 'we can escape the ghouls.'

'What if it's locked?' asked Alice.

'Then,' said Medusa, gathering up her robes, 'as Miss Pinky said: we are lunch.'

14. SINISTER MINISTER

Even in her soaked skinny jeans and squelchy sneakers, Alice managed to sprint at almost Olympic speed. She was the first to make it to the door and threw herself at it with all her force. It opened! Medusa hurtled in next, followed by Miss Pinky. No sooner had they slammed the door shut than the ghouls could be heard scraping at it from the other side, groaning and grunting. Alice could still smell them.

'Yuk!' she said, scrunching her nose. 'That is so disgusting.'

'Can you smell anything else?' asked Medusa.

Alice sniffed the air as she looked around the dimly lit tunnel. 'All I'm getting is ghoul,' she said. 'What should I be smelling for?'

Medusa rummaged in her robes and handed Alice a piece of cloth. 'It is one of Polyphemus's chef's aprons,' she explained.

Alice had seen enough crime dramas to know exactly what Medusa had in mind. 'I'm not a sniffer dog,' she said.

Medusa laid a hand on Alice's arm. 'Please,' she said quietly, 'I must know. Is he here?'

Alice sighed. 'OK, I'll try.' She buried her nose in the apron and breathed in deeply. All sorts of lovely baking smells were ingrained in the cloth: pastry, bread, buttery biscuits. Plus, something really cheesy and salty.

'You are smelling my husband's famous *spanakopita*,' said Medusa, reading her mind again.

'It is a cheese and spinach pastry. Very Greek. Very tasty.'

Alice's mouth watered at the thought of it. Apart from a couple of mouthfuls of Mrs Stuart's revolting porridge, she hadn't eaten today. She sniffed the apron again, then handed it back and stepped further into the tunnel, away from the ghouls scraping at the door. Alice closed her eyes and breathed in. Mostly she could detect musty damp and seaweed, but there was something else mixed in with it. She sniffed again, this time really concentrating. Her eyes sprang open. 'He's here,' she said. 'I'm sure of it.'

Medusa clasped Alice's hands. 'Thank you.'

'No problem,' said Alice, as the door rattled in its frame. 'We'd better keep going.' She looked at Miss Pinky, who was shaking and making lots of different 'I'm scared' faces. 'You OK?'

'Not really,' said Miss Pinky. 'I'm not sure how many of my nine lives I've got left.'

'At least you've got more than one,' said Alice. 'Come on.'

They ran down the tunnel. Medusa's snakes had to curl themselves into a tight knot on top of her head to avoid being hurt by the ceiling, which seemed to get lower the further they went. Finally, they came to another door. Alice tried the handle, but unlike the last one, it was locked. Behind them, a gruesome groaning echoed through the tunnel.

'The ghouls!' shrieked Miss Pinky. 'They're coming!'

The groaning became louder as the creatures staggered around a corner.

Alice winced as she imagined her arm being ripped off and eaten by a ghoul like a chicken drumstick. 'Quick!' she screamed.

Medusa heaved herself into the door, but it didn't budge.

'Let's all try together,' said Alice. 'On three. One. Two. Three!'

CRASH!

The door sprang inwards, sending them flying into a brightly lit room. They ended up in a tangle of arms, legs and snakes, some of which were slithering through Alice's hair. She pushed herself up and shuddered.

'Welcome, ladies. That's quite an entrance.'

Alice turned. A short man with tightly curled black hair was walking towards them. He stopped and smoothed down a lapel on his pinstriped suit.

'You might just have knocked,' said the man, holding out a cane that seemed to be made of ivory. 'Please, let me help you up.'

Alice ignored the cane and got to her feet herself.

The man smiled, his film star-white teeth gleaming. Alice didn't need her super-smellability to detect the litres of aftershave he must have doused his shiny face with.

Behind her, Medusa and Miss Pinky clambered to their feet.

'Gideon Dragstorm!' gasped Miss Pinky.

Medusa's snakes hissed.

'Of course it's me,' laughed the Minister for Monsters. 'Who were you expecting? Father Christmas?'

Alice stared at the minister. What she really needed was a marker pen to draw on some glasses and a moustache so that he matched the photo hanging back in the Jobs4Monsters office. In real life he was almost the same height as her, and Alice could just make out the tips of two smooth brown horns poking through his curls.

'Well,' said the minister, rubbing his hands together, 'this is a pleasure. The actual Medusa, here on my humble little fortress island.' He took a step closer, craning his neck to inspect her. 'Finally, I get to meet the superstar monster herself. I knew if I kidnapped your oaf of a husband, you wouldn't be far behind.'

'It *was* you!' exclaimed Miss Pinky. 'You should be ashamed of yourself! Minister for Monsters, my mermaid's bottom! Minister for Mischief more like.'

Dragstorm flashed another bleached-teeth smile. 'Oh, I'm much more than that,' he said, twirling his cane like a majorette's baton. 'What do you think of this? It's unicorn ivory. They're devilishly hard to hunt down, and you need a power saw to cut off their horns, but it's worth the effort.' Alice shuddered, glad she hadn't touched the cane.

The monstrous moaning of the ghouls

reverberated from the tunnel and a second later, they piled into the room – black-fingernailed hands groping for flesh to rip to shreds, grey lips dribbling over stumpy black teeth.

Quick as a flash, Dragstorm drew a gun out of his jacket and aimed it at the drooling ghouls. 'Now, now, boys,' he said, 'you know the drill.' A fork of lightning shot out of the gun, lassoing the ghouls into a jittering, slobbering huddle. He herded them out of the room and slammed the door shut. 'That'll keep them away for a bit,' he said. 'Took me a while to train them. Turns out, ghouls just hate to be electrocuted.'

'You're supposed to be the minister *for* monsters,' Alice said, 'not *against* them.'

Dragstorm sneered at her. 'Don't tell me you actually want to be ripped to pieces by a ghoul, because that can be arranged.'

Alice gritted her teeth and threw a glare missile in Dragstorm's direction.

'Didn't think so,' he said, pointing the taser gun at them. 'No, I treat every monster equally. I hate them all.' He shot a beady-eyed stare at Alice. 'And I'm not too keen on children, either.'

Keeping the gun trained on them with one hand, Dragstorm swept the other round the room. 'Do you like my little fortress? It's my kidnap command centre.'

Next to Alice, Medusa's snakes were going crazy, whipping around and hissing menacingly.

'But why do you hate monsters?' asked Alice. 'You're a monster, too.'

Dragstorm screwed up his face and spat on the floor. 'Fauns aren't monsters!'

'They are according to your ministry's guidebook,' said Alice. 'It says that you're a Category One monster.'

'Pah!' Dragstorm whacked his cane against the wall. 'Nobody wants to be in Category One. We can't fly, transform, breathe fire, or,' he continued, glaring at Medusa, 'petrify anything.'

'But you're expert pipe players and mountain climbers,' said Alice. 'Those are both useful skills.'

Dragstorm's hand hovered over his taser and he took a step towards her. 'Ask your slithery friend if she'd be content if her only power was puffing into a piccolo,' he snarled.

'At least you're permitted to use your talents,' said Medusa calmly. 'I am forbidden.'

'But you're the Minister for Monsters,' said Alice. 'Doesn't that make you the most powerful monster of all?'

Dragstorm grinned. 'Yes, it does rather. I can change laws like that!' he said, clicking his fingers. 'I can put you out of your jobs and I can have you arrested and thrown into MonsterMax.' He sighed. 'I've done all of those things, but still nobody fears me. So I decided to steal one of the most dangerous monsters there is. I'll admit, he made things slightly more complicated by not attending my fake examination, but I got him in the end. And if that doesn't get the other monsters' attention, just wait till he's found guilty of going AWOL. Imagine! A Category Five monster deserting his post. It's almost worth bringing back the death penalty for punishment.' Dragstorm's eyes widened. 'I think I will,' he said, smiling.

Medusa's snakes went into overdrive, hissing louder than ever.

'Do it, Medusa,' snarled Miss Pinky. 'Use your eyes.'

Dragstorm laughed and twirled the taser gun round his finger like a cowboy with a pistol. Then he reached into his jacket pocket and pulled out a pair of mirrored glasses, just like Medusa's. 'My insurance policy,' he said, putting them on. 'Any attempt to zap me with your eyes, Medusa, will reflect off these and petrify your two friends.' He circled them slowly, not even flinching when Medusa's snakes snapped at his head. Then he went to his desk and pressed a button. 'Security to my office,' he barked.

Seconds later a door on the other side of the room opened and a trio of guards trooped in. At least, Alice *guessed* they were guards. All three of them – two male, one female – were dressed identically in grey boiler suits. As they approached, one of them smiled. His teeth were jagged little pins and when Alice looked closely at his eyes, she saw two glistening, inky-black marbles.

'Selkies,' said Miss Pinky, under her breath. 'I might have guessed.'

Dragstorm clapped his hands. 'Search these prisoners and then take them away,' he said, looking at his watch. 'Next feeding time, throw them to the kraken.'

15. DOG WHISPERING

The selkies wasted no time frisking them, forcing Miss Pinky and Medusa to hand over their mobiles. One of the guards crushed Medusa's phone with a well-aimed stomp, whilst another threw Miss Pinky's against the wall.

'No!' wailed Miss Pinky, as it smashed into pieces. 'That was a new model!'

'**Quiet!**' ordered the third selkie guard, as they were shoved into another dimly lit tunnel. 'You won't be making any more calls today – or any other day.'

There was a stink of damp, unwashed towels and stagnant water in the tunnel, which Alice decided was the selkies' body odour. She tried to ignore it and concentrated instead on not stubbing her toes on the uneven stone floor as they were herded along in the dark.

'Like I always say,' said Miss Pinky, 'never trust a selkie.'

'Silence!' shouted one of the creatures. 'The kraken is always hungry. We can easily bring feeding time forward.'

Alice gulped nervously. First ghouls had tried to eat them for lunch, and now it sounded like a sea monster was going to eat them for its tea.

'Do not fear,' whispered Medusa. 'They wouldn't dare carry out Dragstorm's threat.'

'What's that, snake-head?' snapped another guard, baring its razor-edge teeth. 'Of course we'd dare. It's always fun watching the kraken eat – especially when it plays with its food first.'

They walked on in silence, taking a left here, a right there, until the selkies stopped them in front of a massive wooden door. It had rusty metal hinges and an ancient-looking lock.

'Right,' said one of the selkies, 'here's the dungeon. You'll be nice and comfy in there.'

'Not!' sniggered another.

'Oh, and don't upset the hellhound,' said the third. 'If you try anything funny, he'll rip you to shreds.'

Alice's heart practically jumped out of her mouth. *A hellhound!* It didn't take a genius to guess that it must be a really, utterly, terrifying dog. This was her worst nightmare.

'Do not worry, Alice,' said Medusa. 'Even Dragstorm can't have found a hellhound.'

'Oh, really?' said a selkie, rattling a bunch of keys. 'Here, doggy, doggy. We've got new playmates for you.'

A low growl came from the other side of the door. Alice's skin prickled and her hands went clammy. Then a deeper, longer growl made Alice's chest vibrate. She tried to breathe but couldn't seem to fill her lungs.

A DOG! WHY DID IT HAVE TO BE A DOG?

She almost thought about making a run for it, but it was too late, because the key-jangling selkie had already unlocked the door. Before Alice knew what was happening, she was pushed into the dungeon with Medusa and Miss Pinky. She turned to try and escape, but the door was slammed in her face.

Then, from somewhere behind her, came a menacing growl, followed by a single, from-the-depths-of-hell bark.

Alice didn't dare move so much as an eyelash. If this had been a game of musical statues, she'd be the undisputed winner. The only sound in the dungeon, apart from the blood pumping in her head, was heavy panting. It sounded like an old steam train slowly building up power, getting ready to pull away from the station, or in this case, pounce for the kill. Maybe if they stayed rooted to the spot for long enough, the hellhound would lose interest in them. It was pitch dark in the dungeon, so the creature wouldn't be able to see them. *But*, thought Alice, *it will be able to* smell *us*. She could certainly smell it: ten parts dog and a million parts blood and guts!

So, this was how she was going to die: not chomped to pieces in the water by the kraken, but torn to shreds in the dark by a hellhound. As the creature's dog breath wafted over her, she clenched her fists, toes and teeth.

'Please don't eat us,' she found herself saying in as calm a voice as she could manage. 'We want to be friends.'

Next to her, Miss Pinky made a tiny mewing noise like a kitten stuck on a window ledge. The hellhound growled again. This time, Alice could feel its hot breath on her face. How big *was* this thing? Judging by the heavy thumps she could hear approaching, it was **ginormous**. And then, before she even had time to scream, she was pushed back against the door, pinned in place by both shoulders. Something that felt like a warm, wet dishcloth started slopping and slapping her cheeks.

'It's eating someone!' cried Miss Pinky.

Alice gasped for breath between the hellhound's slobbering tongue licks. But whilst the animal soaked her cheeks and filled her ears with its drool, she felt certain it wouldn't bite her. How she knew this was a mystery. It wasn't like she'd had any dog-handling experience – not even with Grandad Bertie's Jackahuahua!

'Good doggy,' she managed to say. 'Good boy.'

And with that, the licking stopped. Alice felt the hellhound release her and it thumped to the ground by her feet.

'Alice? Are you all right?' asked Medusa.

'Did it eat you?' asked Miss Pinky.

'No,' whispered Alice, 'but I really wish I had a light.'

She felt her satchel moving and a warm yellow glow suddenly filled the area around them. Alice wiped some stringy dog slobber from her eyes.

'Glister! It's you!'

The sprite hummed gently and flitted around the roof.

'Where did that come from?' asked Miss Pinky.

'Balmoral,' said Alice. 'It must have stowed away in my satchel.'

'Go Alice!' Miss Pinky said, laughing. 'You didn't

waste any time getting yourself a monster gadget!'

Glister dropped lower and Alice followed its light to where a massive black dog was slumped on the ground, his tongue lolling from the side of his enormous mouth, two shiny brown eyes twinkling back up at her.

'Hello, Teddy,' she said. 'Thanks for not eating me.'

The hellhound thumped his tail on the ground, making the floor shake, then laid his head on one of his huge paws, which instantly became soaked in a stream of slimy dog drool.

'Teddy?' exclaimed Miss Pinky, who was pressed against the dungeon wall, eyeing the giant dog-monster warily. 'Why are you calling it that? And how did you get it to lie down? And why is it wagging its tail? Hellhounds don't wag their tails, they drink your blood.'

Alice carefully stepped over the dog and turned to Miss Pinky and Medusa. Despite not being able to see the gorgon's eyes, Alice could sense the intensity of her stare.

'I don't know how I know his name, or how I got him to lie down.' She bent down and gave Teddy a quick rub behind his ear. 'But I do know he likes me and that he won't attack us.'

'No way!' cried Miss Pinky. 'You're a dog whisperer!'

Medusa stepped forward. 'Perhaps,' she said. 'But whatever the reason, you have an affinity with this creature. For that, I am grateful.'

'Ditto,' said Miss Pinky. 'Double ditto!'

Alice looked at the mountain of hellhound panting away next to her. He was the size of a grizzly bear, with claws on his paws to match. But unlike a grizzly bear, this animal was a big softie. He was also incredibly smelly, and it wasn't just his doggy breath – appalling whiffs were wafting up from his other end, too.

'Yuk!' Alice said to the creature, who was now snoring, with snot bubbles popping from his flaring nostrils. Alice turned away from the hound and gingerly tested the air. She was out of Teddy's noxious fug but immediately caught the scent of something else. Something a bit . . . cheesy.

'He's in here, Medusa. Polyphemus is in this dungeon.' Alice peered into the shadows. 'Glister, can you ramp up the power for us?'

The sprite, who'd been glowing dimly above them, flickered and buzzed, turning from yellow to bright white, filling the dungeon with its light.

Glister zoomed ahead and Alice and the others followed.

'Wow!' exclaimed Miss Pinky. 'This place is huge!'

The dungeon opened up into a vast, cavern-like

space – perfect for a movie villain's underground command centre. It branched off here and there into dim and dank-looking nooks, whilst thick, rusting chains hung from massive rings fastened to the stone walls.

Glister paused mid-flight and cast a beam into a corner where the rocky roof sloped towards the ground. A pile of grubby white sheets seemed to be wedged in place – it matched the smell of Polyphemus's apron exactly.

'Polyphemus!' cried Medusa. 'Is that you, my sweet?'

The pile grunted, then began shifting and scraping its way out, sending cascades of rock dust showering down. Eventually, it had shunted forward enough to unfold and heave itself up, clambering first to its knees. Then, feeling for some protruding rocks with giant, fat-fingered hands, it pulled itself to its

square, snow-shovel feet.

For a moment, Alice just stared, transfixed by the cyclops's toes, each as large as a marrow. Then she slowly raised her head, taking in the huge bulk of his body. He was dressed in a grubby and torn, oversized chef's outfit – a size XXXXXL. Thick and very dirty arms hung by his sides, whilst his head, covered in a tangled mane of dark hair, towered over Alice. Jug ears stuck out on each side, framing a single, milky-white eye the size of a dinner plate.

'It's me, my sweet Polyphemus. Your Medusa.'

The cyclops's mouth opened first into a gaping hole, then spread wide into a smile full of teeth like broken bricks.

'Meddy!' he roared. **'Can this really be?'**

He held out his huge, muscled arms and Medusa ran into them, craning her long neck up to smother the cyclops's cheeks in kisses. Alice looked away – it was a private moment, after all.

Miss Pinky swabbed her eyes with her sleeve. 'So romantic,' she sobbed.

After kissing and hugging and whispering into each other's ears, Medusa uncoiled herself from Polyphemus's arms, straightened out her snakes and beckoned to Alice and Miss Pinky.

'These are my friends, Polyphemus. Here is Miss Pinky, from Jobs4Monsters.'

Miss Pinky high-fived the cyclops's hand. 'Respect,' she said.

'And this is my new friend, Alice,' said Medusa. 'A brave and determined girl.'

Alice took Polyphemus's thumb and shook it. 'It's wonderful to meet you, sir,' she said. 'But I'm sorry it has to be in a dungeon.'

Polyphemus blinked his eye and nodded. 'Any friend of my wife's is mine also,' he boomed. 'But why are you all in this forsaken place? Did that man kidnap you too?'

'No, my sweet,' said Medusa. 'We came to recue you.'

'Rescue!' thundered Polyphemus. 'You put yourselves in danger for me?'

'You got it,' said Miss Pinky. 'And let me tell you, it has been epic!'

Polyphemus let out an earthquake of a sob. 'I'm sorry,' he cried. 'He tricked me. Told me he needed help with a delivery. I climbed into the lorry and he locked me inside. I tried to get away, but they chained me up.' He lifted a foot and Alice noticed the heavy chain attached to Polyphemus's ankle. His skin was raw and bleeding where he must have tried to break free. 'But what of the hound? How did you get past the beast?'

'Never mind that,' said Medusa, to Alice's relief. She didn't fancy trying to explain how she'd managed to 'talk' to Teddy. 'You look so weak, my darling. Have they even fed you?'

Polyphemus pointed to a bucket. 'I dared not eat their offering,' he said.

Alice picked it up and looked inside. 'Blergh!' she winced, putting it down. 'Fish bits and seaweed.' She looked at everyone. 'Right,' she said. 'How are we going to get out of here?'

Miss Pinky started hopping from paw to paw. 'Before we work that out,' she said, 'I really need to pee. I must have swallowed gallons of seawater earlier on.' She looked round the dungeon. 'Don't suppose this place has a loo?'

Alice handed her the bucket. 'This will have to do.'

Miss Pinky looked inside and gagged. 'No thanks,' she said. 'Those fish heads might bite my bottom. I'll find somewhere private.' She turned and scurried into a dark corner. 'No peeking, all right!'

Moments later a yelp echoed round the dungeon, followed by a grumbling and muttering.

'I wish people wouldn't leave things lying around for prisoners desperate for a pee to trip over,' said Miss Pinky, holding a round object in her hand.

'Don't you mean you wish they wouldn't leave *bits of themselves* lying around?' said Alice.

Miss Pinky looked down at what she was holding. 'Yikes!' she screamed. 'A skull!'

She threw it to Alice, who only just caught it and found herself staring into two empty eye sockets.

'Well, pardon me for dying,' said an indignant-sounding voice.

Alice spun on her heels. 'Who said that?'

Miss Pinky's terrified eyes shone in Glister's light, whilst Medusa shrugged.

'I mean, it's not as if I had much say in the matter,' continued the voice. 'Not everyone gets to die snug in their own beds.'

Alice lifted the skull up and looked underneath it. She peered through its remaining teeth, catching a faint whiff of egg. *What am I doing?!* she thought. As if a skull could talk! But the voice had sounded incredibly close. She looked at the eye sockets again. They'd begun to glow green.

'Er . . . guys,' she said, 'what's going on?' She held the skull out. 'There's something inside it.'

Medusa spoke first. 'Put the skull down, Alice,' she said calmly. 'And step away.'

'Yikes!' shouted Miss Pinky. 'We've got ourselves a poltergeist!'

16. POLTER-HEIST

Before she had a chance to move, the skull began vibrating in Alice's hands. It became warm, then hot, and as she watched – horrified and amazed in equal measure – a jet of green light shot out of its mouth.

The green light shimmered and pulsed for a moment, before forming into the shape of a young man. He had long, straggly hair, and was wearing frayed breeches and what looked like an old sack as a shirt.

The teenaged poltergeist floated in the air, arms crossed and looking annoyed. 'Can't a dead man rest in peace?' he said, in a quivering voice. 'It was dire enough with the comings and goings and to-ings and fro-ings these past few days,' he continued, 'and now someone comes along and kicks me in the head.'

'Soz,' said Miss Pinky. 'I didn't see you.'

The green guy giggled and shimmered out of focus for a second. 'Doesn't matter,' he said. 'I can't feel anything anyway.' He floated over to Alice. 'As long as my home is still in one piece.' He inspected his skull. 'Good,' he said, then floated up level with her eyes. 'And who are you?'

'I'm Alice, and these are my friends.'

The poltergeist flew around, waving at everyone. 'The giant I recognise,' he said. 'You wouldn't believe how loud he snores.'

'I think I might,' said Medusa. 'To me it is like music.'

'If you say so,' said the poltergeist. 'Now, if I could

just remember my own name . . . Am I Phillip . . . or Frederick . . . or maybe Finbar?' He pulled at his knotted hair in frustration. 'Come on, man, it's not that difficult.' Suddenly, his eyes widened. 'Got it!' he cried, zooming around the dungeon like a green laser. He shot towards Alice, disappeared into one of his skull's eye sockets, then burst back out of the other. 'It's Fergus!' he shouted. 'Fergus Fingal! I remembered!'

'And are you a poltergeist?' asked Alice.

Fergus Fingal held up a hand and looked at Alice through it. 'I suppose I must be,' he said. 'I was a person once. Last I remember of that, I was chained up to the wall over there.' He pointed to the dark corner where Miss Pinky had tripped over his skull. 'All I'd done was steal a loaf of bread for my tea. I hadn't eaten for days,' he explained. 'I was going to pay for it eventually.' Fergus shook his head and wiped his nose with the back of his hand. 'Never even got to say a farewell to my mother. They shipped me over here and left me to rot.'

'That's terrible,' said Alice. 'Poor you.'

Fergus stared at Alice mournfully. 'It *has* been rather dull,' he said. 'Hundreds of years with only the rats for company.' Then he smiled. 'But now you're all here, and once you've died long, agonising deaths too, we can dance and skip and fly through the walls together. It's going to be great!'

'Actually,' said Alice, 'do you mind if we don't?'

'I'm with her,' said Miss Pinky, shuddering. 'A long, agonising death is not on my bucket list.'

Fergus shrugged. 'Please yourselves,' he said, and set about flinging himself around the dungeon, humming as he went.

Alice delved into her bag for the *OMG*, calling for Glister to help light the pages.

POLTERGEIST		
CATEGORY:		**2**
AVERAGE LIFE SPAN:		**FOREVER**
HUMAN INTEGRATION:		**YES**
SKILLS:		**SPOOKING; SCARING; MOVING OBJECTS**
RESTRICTIONS:		**POLTERGEISTS MUST REMAIN NEAR THEIR BONES**
DANGER RATING:		**MODERATE**

Alice slipped the book back into her bag whilst her mind whirled with an idea that had suddenly popped into it.

'Hey, Fergus, come over here.'

'Careful, Alice,' said Medusa. 'Poltergeists can be unpredictable.'

'It's OK,' she said. 'I've got this.'

The poltergeist floated over and hovered just in front of her. 'At your service.'

'How would you like to get off this bogging island with us?'

Fergus clasped his hands in front of his shimmering body. 'Oh yes, please!' he cried. 'I dream of poltering my geist somewhere new!' Then his eyes narrowed. 'What do I have to do?'

'Nothing much,' said Alice. 'Just steal some keys.'

Fergus said nothing, but his floating body began shaking. Then it started to expand, turning an even more vivid shade of green. Within seconds he'd tripled in size and a smell like manky lettuce in a salad drawer filled the dungeon. Was this what Medusa had meant by 'unpredictable'? The poltergeist's wild eyes bulged. Then he opened his mouth wider than Alice thought possible as he exploded in rage.

'STEAL? STEALING IS THEFT! LARCENY! PILLAGE! IT IS AN ABOMINATION! THE WORK OF THE DEVIL! GUILTY! GUILTY! GUILTY! TAKE HIM AWAY AND LEAVE HIM TO ROT!'

Just when Alice was certain Fergus's gaping mouth was going to swallow her whole, his ghostly body burst into a fine, green-tinged mist and appeared to evaporate into nothing.

Alice stared into the empty space left behind. Was he dead? Again? Could a poltergeist die twice?

Miss Pinky sighed. 'Typical!' she said. 'They always hog the spotlight, these poltergeists.'

'Will he come back?' asked Alice.

'Oh, he'll be back. He won't be able to resist the attention.'

Sure enough, seconds later, a thin green cloud appeared, quickly transforming into Fergus's shape. 'I do apologise,' he said, back to his normal voice. 'I don't know what came over me. For a moment I was back in the courtroom being sentenced.' He shuddered then smiled at Alice. 'So, you want me to pinch some keys?'

Before Alice could answer, Medusa stepped forward. 'What is it you have planned, Alice?'

'Escape, of course,' said Alice.

Miss Pinky laughed. 'Yeah, right! We're just going to walk out and breeze past a hundred hungry ghouls and a load of sadistic selkies?'

Alice threw Miss Pinky an especially annoyed glare-bomb. 'If we do nothing, Dragstorm's going to either throw us in MonsterMax or, more likely, feed us to this kraken. I don't think we have a choice.'

'But aren't you scared?' asked Miss Pinky, looking like a spooked kitten.

'Yes, I'm scared,' said Alice. 'I've been scared loads of times in the last two days. I've had to face my worst phobias one after the other: I've had to fly, and I've been up close and way too personal with snakes. No offence, Medusa.'

'None taken,' said the gorgon.

'And I've made friends with a hellhound when I'm supposed to be terrified of dogs.' As if on cue, Teddy lumbered across the dungeon, wagging his tail so fast it made Medusa's robes billow up around her legs. 'Two days ago,' continued Alice, 'my life was kind of boring. Now it's not. Monsters are awesome. You are all amazing. I want my life to have monsters in it. Actually, I want to have my life, and I'm not sure Dragstorm is going to let me keep it. So, I'm getting out of this dungeon, no matter what's out there.'

'Stop,' blubbed Miss Pinky, dabbing her eyes with her sleeve. 'I'm welling up.'

'Me too,' said Fergus, 'and I'm not sure I can even cry.'

'So, it's either rot away in here like poor Fergus did, or try to escape,' said Alice, wiping the water that kept dripping from the rocks above off her face.

Nobody said anything, and then Teddy barked.

'Thank you, Teddy,' said Alice. 'Anyone else coming with me?'

Polyphemus grunted from his spot by the wall. 'Yes please,' he boomed. 'If you can get these chains off.'

Medusa took her husband's hand and reached for Alice's. 'With bravery like yours, Alice, how can we fail?'

'I think failure's still very much a possibility,' said Miss Pinky. 'But if we do get out, I'll be a huge monstamedia star. So, count me in!'

'Excellent!' Alice beckoned Fergus down from the ceiling where he was turning somersaults. 'Will you get the keys?'

'Oh, go on! Why not? If you promise to find me a new home.'

'Deal!' Alice tried to high five the poltergeist but ending up just waving her hand through his body.

She held her satchel open and dropped his skull inside. 'When we get off this island, you're coming too,' she said.

Fergus cheered and clasped his hands together. 'Thank you!' he cried. 'Now, where shall I find these keys?'

'One of the selkies has them,' said Alice.

'What does it look like?' asked the poltergeist.

Miss Pinky snarled. 'Beady eyes, bad teeth, fishy breath.'

The poltergeist wrinkled his nose. 'Anything else I can do for you? Throw a chair? Smash a mirror? Pull someone's nose hairs?'

'None of that,' said Alice. 'Just the keys.'

Fergus puffed out his chest. 'Consider it done,' he said proudly, before whizzing off through the door.

They only had to wait a minute or so before the poltergeist shot back into the dungeon, coughing

and wheezing like he'd just run a marathon. 'Got
them,' he panted, jingling a set of keys in the air.
'Stupid selkie was so busy scoffing down a bowl of
fish flakes, it didn't even notice me lifting them.'

Alice took the keys and headed straight for
Polyphemus. 'Time you were set free,' she said,

crouching down and unlocking his shackles. Having released him, she threw the keys to Miss Pinky. 'Can you open the door?'

'With pleasure,' said Miss Pinky.

'Take care to be quiet,' ordered Medusa, who was guiding Polyphemus out of his corner.

'Hey, chill out. I'm not a total butterfingers, you know,' said Miss Pinky, instantly dropping the keys to the stone floor with a loud clatter.

Everyone froze.

'Oops!' exclaimed Miss Pinky. 'Silly me.' She padded to the door and carefully inserted the largest key into the lock, turning it slowly until it clunked open. 'There,' she said, pushing the massive door outwards. 'I'm not completely useless after all!'

Alice and Miss Pinky stepped out into the tunnel. Teddy followed, snuffling and panting, and next flittered Glister, humming. Fergus chose to float through the wall and then they all waited for Medusa to lead her husband through the doorway.

'Over to you, Alice,' said the gorgon, looking up and down the tunnel. 'Which direction smells the safest?'

'Great,' moaned Alice. 'So now I've got to sniff our way to freedom?'

17. UNCOOL GHOULS

Alice closed her eyes and breathed in deeply. Then she did the same facing the opposite way.

'Well?' asked Medusa.

Alice shrugged. She sniffed the air again in both directions. 'Down that way,' she said, 'I'm picking up seaweed, salt, damp rock and a sort of fishy smell.' She couldn't quite place it, but it reminded her of the sushi conveyor belt restaurant at the shopping mall. 'The way we came in,' she said, wrinkling her nose, 'I smell selkies.'

'Are you sure?' asked Medusa.

'Yes,' said Alice, nodding vigorously. She'd never

forget their putrid fish-stink breath.

'So,' said Miss Pinky, 'one way it's unidentified fishiness, and the other it's easily identified fishiness.'

'Maybe we should go that way,' said Alice, pointing up the tunnel. 'Better the devil – or selkie – you know.'

Miss Pinky shrieked, quickly covering her mouth when Medusa hissed at her to be quiet. 'No way,' she whispered. 'I'm not having their teeth shred me to cat mince.'

'I agree with Miss Pinky,' said Medusa. 'Dragstorm's bound to be lurking in his office. We should head down the tunnel. Remember, this is an old war fortress – there will be more than one entrance.'

'OK,' said Alice, wishing she liked sushi. If she'd ever eaten it, she might have been able to tell whether the smell coming from the other end of the tunnel was raw squid. Raw, as in, still very much alive.

'All paths are dangerous,' said Medusa, gently touching Alice's arm. 'Our success depends on how we choose to confront the danger.'

The escape party headed down into the damp depths of the fortress. Every so often, they had to help Polyphemus through the narrowest sections. His bare arms were soon streaked with blood where the rocks had scraped his skin.

'What a stupid place to hide a cyclops,' puffed Miss Pinky, as she and Alice pushed the giant's bottom to help him squeeze past two massive boulders. 'Don't even think about farting, mister, because we're right in the toxic zone back here. Ouch!' She tripped as the cyclops shot out the other side. As Alice leaned down to help Miss Pinky up, a gruesome groan echoed up from somewhere ahead and an unmistakable stink of rotting flesh wafted towards them.

'No!' cried Alice. **'Ghouls.'**

'Yeah, a whole garrison of ghouls by the sound of it,' said Miss Pinky. 'We don't stand a chance.'

'Nonsense,' snapped Medusa. 'Time for tactics.'

'We have tactics?'

'Yes, Miss Pinky, we do.' Medusa looked at everyone in turn. 'To survive these ghouls, we must play to our strengths and accept our weaknesses. Teddy, Polyphemus and I are the strongest, so we will lead. Miss Pinky and Alice, you are the weakest, so we will shield you.'

'Excellent tactics,' said Miss Pinky.

'Can't I help?' asked Alice. 'There must be something I can do.'

'Of course there is,' said Medusa. 'You must remind Teddy that he is a true hellhound and that the ghouls are his enemy.'

'OK,' said Alice, thinking how weird it was that

an hour ago she'd never been near a dog, and now she was talking to a monster hound. How was it he understood her and no one else?

'Do not concern yourself with that,' said Medusa. 'Now is not the time.'

Maybe not, thought Alice, bending down to whisper into Teddy's ear, *but I need answers when this is all over.*

Having received his instructions, Teddy padded out in front, flanked by Polyphemus and Medusa. Alice and Miss Pinky slipped in behind, whilst Fergus and Glister floated above, ready to distract the ghouls any way they could. They'd taken up this formation just in time, because seconds later, a mass of ghouls, all goggling eyes and groping fingers, appeared round the next corner.

Teddy instantly launched his immense body at the first few, grabbing them in his gnashing jaws. His murderous growls seemed to penetrate Alice's chest as he thrashed around. Now she truly understood how this monster had got its name.

Polyphemus and Medusa were fighting ghouls, too. The cyclops roared as he smashed heads into rocks and ripped arms from sockets. Medusa's snakes swirled and snapped, tearing flesh from bone. Green-white flashes filled the tunnel like strobe lights as Fergus and Glister zipped around causing high-voltage chaos.

'Duck!' screamed Miss Pinky, as an arm flew overhead.

'Watch out!' yelled Alice as a ghoul's head almost smashed into her own. Stooping to miss the shower of assorted body parts, she tripped over a discarded leg, dragging Miss Pinky down with her. By the time they'd both clambered back to their feet, their protective shield had continued down the tunnel, leaving them totally exposed.

'Quick!' shouted Alice. 'Back into position!'

They began to run, dodging ghoul debris as it rained down. They almost made it. But then, like a scene from a really bad horror movie, two ghouls suddenly stepped out of the shadows and blocked their path.

"GRAAARGHH! GLEEERPHH!"

"GRUUURCHH!

GLAAARFHH!"

Their stumpy teeth gnashed together, spraying bloody phlegm everywhere.

'Medusa!' cried Alice. 'Help!' But it was no use. The others were all busy fighting ghouls. She and Miss Pinky were on their own.

They lunged forward, each shoving a ghoul in the

chest. For a moment, the creatures looked confused, saliva dribbling from their lips, but it didn't take them long to recover. The ghouls threw their arms forward again. One tangled its long, manky fingernails in Alice's hair, breathing its foul death stench in her face. Out of the corner of her eye, Alice saw Miss Pinky tackle the other one to the ground. Pushing the ghoul away from her face with one hand, Alice stuck her other hand inside her satchel. The monster gnashed its blackened teeth. She heard its gasping, rasping breath as she rummaged desperately in her bag.

The ghoul lunged forward to bite her. Just in time, Alice's hand found what it was feeling for.

'Take that!' she screamed, jamming the *OMG* between the ghoul's jaws. It staggered backwards, drool flooding from its gaping mouth. Quick as a flash, Miss Pinky sprang off the ghoul she'd pinned to the

ground, and with both booted paws outstretched, she slammed into Alice's attacker.

'Yah! Ker-pow!'

The creature sprawled back, hitting the wall and then landing in a heap on top of its comatose friend.

'Nice book work, Alice,' panted Miss Pinky.

'Great boot action, Miss Pinky,' puffed Alice.

'No point in watching hours of online monster wrestling videos if you can't learn a few moves yourself,' said Miss Pinky, wiping some ghoul drool off her whiskers.

Alice laughed. 'Is there anything you can't learn from the internet?'

'Not that I know of,' Miss Pinky said, brushing off her boots. 'We make an awesome team, by the way.'

'The best,' said Alice, smiling at her. 'And talking of the team, where is the rest of it?'

They peered up the eerily quiet tunnel. 'We'd

better find them,' said Alice, beginning to pick her way through the carnage.

Just round the next bend they found Polyphemus slumped against the tunnel wall, fishing bits of skin and flesh out of his hair. Teddy was lying on the floor panting, blood dripping from his fangs, and two of Medusa's snakes were licking her sunglass lenses clean with their forked tongues.

'WE DID IT! HURRAY! WE'VE SAVED THE DAY!' sang Fergus, bouncing off the walls. He stopped to catch his breath. 'Actually,' he said, 'I need a rest.' And with that, he turned into a thin green wisp and disappeared into Alice's satchel.

'What happened?' asked Medusa, striding forward. 'Where were you?'

'Ghoul ambush,' explained Alice.

'No biggie,' said Miss Pinky.

'Very well,' said Medusa. 'If we have caught our

breath, we should continue.' She reached down to help Polyphemus to his feet and then swished away.

'I don't know about you,' grumbled Miss Pinky as they continued down the sloping tunnel, 'but it feels like we're just going deeper inside the fortress. And it's getting pretty wet.'

'Mmm,' said Alice, splashing through a puddle. She'd already worked out that if there was an escape route out of these slippery, dripping tunnels, it was probably going to involve swimming. She decided it was best not to freak out Miss Pinky with *that* piece of news right now.

Pausing for a moment to check the air, Alice detected a strong scent of sea water. Not the fermenting seaweed stench that oozed out of the rock walls, but the fresh, waves-crashing-on-the-shore smell of the ocean.

'Hold up!' she shouted, twitching her nose to try

and pinpoint the scent. 'Through there,' she finally said, pointing to a hole hacked out of the rock.

'Silence!' commanded Medusa.

Everyone obeyed. Even Teddy stopped panting long enough for the sound of lapping water to reach their ears.

Alice shivered. It was either excitement, hope, terror or dread. Deciding to go with the first two options, she opened her satchel and took out the skull. 'Wakey, wakey, Fergus Fingal.'

The poltergeist swirled out like a green candle flame. 'I was just getting settled in there,' he said. 'By the way, I feel I should point out that there's a manky hanky at the bottom of your bag.'

'Never mind that,' said Alice. 'Can you and Glister go and see what's through there?'

Fergus bowed his head. 'At your service.' He giggled, following the sprite as it flickered through the gap.

Moments later Fergus steamed back out, trailing green smoke in his wake.

'There's a way out!' he said excitedly. 'And best of all,' continued the poltergeist, 'there's nothing guarding it. Come on!'

With all thoughts of terror and dread wiped away, Alice followed Fergus through the gap, feeling her way along a short passage until it opened up on to a cavern with a huge pool. Glister shimmered overhead, his light reflecting off the water's surface. At the far end of the pool was a large, round gate made up of criss-crossing metal bars. And waves were splashing through it from the sea!

'Yes!' Alice shouted, as Miss Pinky joined her. The hellhound padded to her side and licked her hand. 'Look, Teddy,' she said, 'that's our way out.'

While Medusa struggled to help Polyphemus through the jagged entrance to the cavern, Alice walked over to the pool to investigate. Bubbles were breaking on the surface of the water. She looked up to where Fergus was floating. 'Did you check *under* the water?'

'Let me think,' said the poltergeist, inserting a finger inside his head. 'No. I don't believe I did.'

With dread and terror very much back in her mind, Alice slowly looked down at the pool. The bubbles were rising in a steady stream, like air from a snorkel. The water began to ripple, then started simmering like a pan of potatoes about to boil over.

Miss Pinky mewed quietly. 'Is that the—?'

Before Alice even had a chance to scream, a wriggling, writhing tentacle shot out through the water's churning surface. It whipped along the ground and lassoed her ankle in a rubbery, blubbery twist.

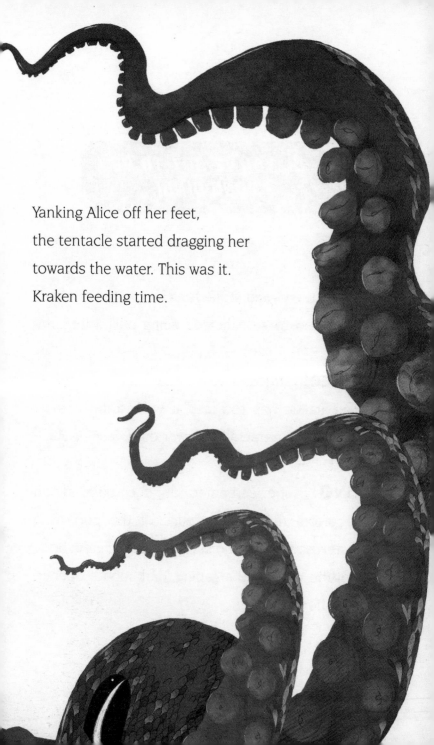

Yanking Alice off her feet,
the tentacle started dragging her
towards the water. This was it.
Kraken feeding time.

18. YOU'VE GOT TO BE SQUIDDING!

Alice felt the jagged stone floor slice into her hands as she tried to stop herself being pulled into the pool.

'Alice!' shrieked Miss Pinky, reaching for her.

The kraken was too fast. It yanked its tentacle back in like a retractable power cord, lashing Alice around.

'No!' she screamed as she skidded on her bottom right to the edge of the pool. The monster squid had hoisted its huge, grey body out of the water and a gaping, dark mouth opened to suck her in . . .

And then the tentacle released its grip and the creature sploshed back into the pool, dumping Alice in a quivering, shivering heap on the side. For a split second, she stared into the kraken's shimmering, oil-slick eyes before they disappeared under the surface. Alice scrambled to her feet but slipped on the slimy stone floor. As she crashed back down to the ground, Fergus's skull rolled out of her satchel and plopped into the water.

'MY HEAD!' screamed the poltergeist.

Alice watched helplessly as the skull bobbed on the water. The monster rose up again, its skin pulsing with waves of rainbow-coloured light right down to the ends of its coiling tentacles. It reminded Alice of the tiny deep-sea creatures she'd once seen on a nature programme – except a million times bigger. Then, one of its tentacles wound around the skull and dragged it down into the depths of the pool.

'No!' wailed Fergus.

Miss Pinky and Medusa rushed over to Alice. 'Careful,' she said, as they helped her up, 'we mustn't scare it.'

'What do you mean, "mustn't scare *it*"!' gasped Miss Pinky. 'I couldn't be more scared if a giant fire-breathing dragon grabbed me in its claws and tried to feed me to its hatchlings.'

As they backed away from the pool, the tentacle holding the skull shot out of the water. It let go, and the skull sailed through the air. Without thinking, Alice reached up and caught it.

'Nice save!' said Miss Pinky.

'I'll second that!' said Fergus, hovering overhead. 'Without my skull I would disappear forever.'

Alice shook some water out of the eye sockets and was about to put the skull back in her bag when the tentacle reached out of the water and tapped it lightly with its tip. Then it pulled back and slapped the surface of the water, its suckers pulsating and squelching.

'Curious behaviour,' said Medusa.

'You're not kidding,' said Miss Pinky. 'That thing could have eaten us by now. It mustn't be hungry.'

'It's smaller than I thought it would be,' said Medusa.

Alice stared at the writhing and waggling tentacle. It seemed eager – as if it wanted something from her. Suddenly, she realised what it was. She held the skull out towards the pool. 'Here, boy! Or girl! Or whatever!'

'No!' yelled the poltergeist, floating above her and waving his arms in protest.

'Sorry, Fergus,' said Alice, 'but I think the kraken wants to play.' Then, ignoring Fergus's screams, she threw his skull to the kraken. **'Catch!'**

A tentacle caught the skull in its squelching suckers, and instantly launched it back towards Alice's waiting hands. Fergus zipped back and forth in the air, following his skull as Alice and the kraken played catch. When the kraken had finally tired of the game, its tentacle dropped the skull on the side of the pool, by Alice's feet. She quickly put it back in her satchel.

'I can't believe you just played a game of catch with a kraken,' said Miss Pinky.

'I can't believe you just played a game of catch with my skull!' shrieked Fergus.

'If I hadn't seen this with my own eyes,' said Medusa, 'I would never have believed it.'

Alice approached the edge of the pool again and kneeled down. She plunged her hand into the water and began stroking one of the kraken's tentacles. The rainbow shimmers went into overdrive, zapping across the creature's body like some sort of power surge.

'You're just a baby, aren't you?' said Alice. 'Did that nasty man take you away from your mummy?'

The kraken stared at Alice for a moment and blinked very slowly, then turned away sadly and sank to the bottom of the pool.

Medusa joined Alice by the pool's edge and placed an arm around her shoulder. 'I have seen many wonderful things in my long lifetime,' she said, 'but I have never witnessed bravery such as yours. The kraken is feared by every living soul, apart, it seems, from you, Alice.'

'I still can't believe you used my skull like that,' said Fergus, looking peeved.

'I'm sorry,' said Alice, 'but we needed to make friends with the kraken. And anyway,' she continued, tapping her satchel, 'you're still in one piece.'

'Actually,' came a sharp voice from behind them, 'none of you will be in one piece for much longer.'

Alice smelled selkie skin. Compared to the kraken's sushi-fresh scent, the guards reeked of way-past-its-sell-by-date fish pie.

Teddy barked, the deep sound amplified by the cavern. Alice sensed the hellhound was about to pounce, but then he whimpered as the unmistakable noise of selkie teeth rasping against each other ripped through the air.

'How sweet,' mocked a selkie, 'the ickle poochy woochy is scared of the sealy wealies.'

Teddy cowered and hid behind Alice's legs.

Five selkies leered at them, their teeth glistening like knife points in Glister's light.

'Aren't you lot clever?' said one of the guards. 'Taming the hellhound and breaking out of the dungeon. Dragstorm's not going to like this one bit.'

'Is that so?' said Alice, hearing a gentle sloshing in the water behind her. If she was right, the kraken had resurfaced.

'Yes, missy,' snarled the guard, 'it is. Now, you either come quietly, or you come in pieces.' The selkies gnashed their teeth together. Being caught in them would be like being trapped inside an industrial meat slicing machine.

'We're not going anywhere with you,' she said, trying to ignore their razor-sharp mouths.

'Thought you'd say that.' The selkie yelped once, and his fellow guards yelped back. Then, teeth gleaming, they pounced.

Alice whistled and shouted, 'Here, Squiddy! Playtime!'

A mass of writhing tentacles flew out of the pool and over everyone's heads.

'Duck!' screamed Alice, as the tentacles whipped

this way and that, spraying water all over the cavern. She and Miss Pinky crouched down, as Medusa helped Polyphemus take cover.

Alice watched as the kraken's tentacles twisted around the selkies, dragging them kicking and squealing to the pool. The kraken spouted a huge fountain of water, then pulled the selkies under the surface in a wild confusion of thrashing and foaming.

'Epic!' said Miss Pinky, grinning from whisker to whisker.

'That was indeed astonishing,' said Medusa, wiping her glasses.

'Is everyone still alive?' roared Polyphemus.

'Yes!' shouted Alice. She turned to the churning water, which looked a bit like a piranha feeding frenzy. The kraken seemed to be enjoying its selkie playdate and flung the guards around the pool like helpless ragdolls. *I guess he likes to play rough,*

thought Alice, ducking to avoid getting splashed as the kraken threw a terrified-looking selkie into the air and caught it again in his tentacle.

'Thank you!' she said, hoping the giant squid could hear her. 'Come on then,' she said to everyone else. 'Let's get that gate open before Dragstorm works out he's lost his guards.'

She ran over to the end of the pool.

'It looks really heavy,' she said, examining the gate. There seemed to be some sort of pulley mechanism attached, and metal tracks which ran up to the roof of the cavern.

'It's like a castle portcullis,' said Medusa, studying the dark, rocky wall. 'Glister, would you shine a light over here please?'

The sprite directed a beam of light towards the wall.

'There!' Medusa pointed to a rusty metal wheel which was connected by a chain to the gate. She grabbed the wheel and attempted to turn it. 'Impossible,' she said. 'This requires the strength of a giant.'

'Well, that's lucky,' said Miss Pinky, 'because we've got one of those right here!'

'Come, my sweet Polyphemus.' Medusa directed the cyclops's hands to the wheel. 'Let us pray to

Zeus that you still have the power within you.'

Polyphemus braced his legs, gritted his broken-brick teeth, and heaved against the wheel. His arm muscles bulged, and his face turned beetroot red. Just when Alice thought the vein in his neck would burst and splatter them all with cyclops blood, the wheel shifted and the gate slowly began to rise from the water.

'That's it!'
'Keep going!'
'Nice one!'

Everyone shouted words of encouragement as Polyphemus struggled with the wheel, cranking it round centimetre by centimetre. The gate clanked and rattled as it screeched its way up the track, metal grating on metal. Finally, with Polyphemus panting and gasping for breath, the gate had lifted clear of the water. Beyond it was the sea!

'Everyone in the water!' shouted Alice.

'What?' screamed Miss Pinky.

Alice grabbed her friend's hand. 'You know that bit of you that's more mermaid than cat?'

'Yes.'

'Channel it right now,' said Alice.

Miss Pinky bit her bottom lip. 'I'm scared.'

'We all are,' said Alice, preparing to jump in. 'Hold on! What about Polyphemus?'

The cyclops was still holding the wheel, sweat pouring in huge beads from his forehead.

'Go!' he boomed. 'I must hold this wheel.'

'We can't leave you behind!' yelled Alice.

'I shall remain with my husband,' said Medusa.

'No way!' Alice stamped her foot. 'We can't leave anyone behind.' She stared into the frothing, bubbling pool. 'Squiddy!' she shouted. 'Help us!'

A second later, two tentacles burst out of the

water, each holding a gasping selkie in its coiled tip. The tentacles thrust upwards towards the gate and wedged the selkies in the tracks either side.

'Let go, Polyphemus!' yelled Alice.

The cyclops released his grip on the wheel. The gate dropped slightly, then stuck fast, as the selkies let out high-pitched squeals. Alice winced, but there wasn't time to feel sorry for the guards.

'*Now*, everyone in the water!' she shouted, grabbing Miss Pinky's hand and pulling her into the pool.

'Arghh!' screamed Miss Pinky, craning her neck to keep her head above the surface. 'Why did you do that?'

'So you didn't have time to panic,' said Alice, swimming towards the exit. 'Hey! Get off!'

Fergus had landed on her head and draped his ghostly green legs around her shoulders.

'I couldn't swim when I was alive,' said Fergus, 'so I doubt I can swim now I'm dead.'

'You're a poltergeist,' spluttered Alice. 'If you can float through walls, you can probably float on the water.'

'Perhaps,' said Fergus, 'but I'm not taking any chances.'

As Glister flitted ahead to light the way, Alice heard Teddy flop into the water, which sent a mini tsunami sloshing out of the pool. This was followed by a second massive wave as Polyphemus jumped in. Medusa was last to enter the water. Then they all began to swim across the pool, trying to avoid the kraken's over-enthusiastic tickle fight with the three remaining selkies.

'I totally . . . thought . . . you were . . . kraken food . . . back there,' spluttered Miss Pinky between mouthfuls of water as she attempted to kitty paddle.

'You're . . . the bravest . . . human . . . I know.'

'I'm the only human you know,' said Alice, thinking how hard it was to swim whilst fully clothed and with a poltergeist clinging to your back. 'But thanks anyway.'

Just then, Teddy ploughed past, performing a turbo-charged doggy paddle. Barking loudly, he swam through the gateway and out to the open sea.

'Follow Teddy!' shouted Alice. 'Come on, people! Swim!'

19. SOLID AS A ROCK

The instant everyone had swum through the gateway, the kraken yanked the selkies out and sent the gate crashing back down.

'Thank you!' shouted Alice, over the noise of the waves. 'We'll get you out of there soon!'

Swimming away from the cave, Alice squinted as the sun glinted on the water. She breathed in deeply, filling her lungs with the fresh, salty air.

'Can you see someplace for us to come ashore?' she asked Fergus, trying to see over the tops of the waves. The poltergeist floated off Alice's head.

'Over there!' called Fergus, pointing to a stony

beach in the distance.

Alice kicked out, calling to the others to follow her. It wasn't far, but the waves and random currents made swimming much harder. At one point, Alice felt something wrap around her leg. For a split second, she wondered if it was the kraken's mother, but then realised it was only a long piece of seaweed.

Teddy powered on ahead, letting Miss Pinky cling to his neck. Medusa sculled along elegantly on her back, keeping her snakes clear of the water, whilst Polyphemus made use of his height by striding through the waves to freedom.

Just when Alice thought her waterlogged satchel and saturated jeans and sneakers would drag her down to the seabed, they reached the rocky shore.

'I wouldn't if I were you,' sneered a voice from above.

Treading water, Alice looked up. Standing atop

a narrow rock was the Minister for Monsters, his mirrored sunglasses shining brightly in the setting sun.

And he wasn't alone.

Swarming above his head was his squadron of fixies.

'If any of you dare to crawl ashore,' shouted Dragstorm, 'these adorable little monsters will attack.'

In response to the minister's threat, the fixies re-formed into the outline

of a giant wasp, buzzing menacingly. One of them broke away and dive-bombed towards Alice. It hovered just above her head, its green wings beating furiously. This close, Alice could make out two steak knife-sharp fangs in the corners of its tiny mouth, and the metal spurs it wore on its boots. The fixie swiped a foot over her head, slicing off a lock of her hair which fell into the water and floated off. 'Hey!' shouted Alice. 'I don't want a haircut.'

As the fixie flew back to regroup with the rest of the evil critters, Dragstorm continued to taunt them. 'Well, this is fun. I wonder how long you can stay afloat for.'

Alice was wondering the same thing herself. She grabbed hold of one of Teddy's paws as he floated past with Miss Pinky hanging on to his neck.

'I wish I was more of a mermaid,' Miss Pinky moaned.

'I wish I was even a tiny bit mermaid,' said Alice.

'Did someone say mermaid?' came a voice from across the water.

Over the wind, Alice suddenly heard the sound of someone singing.

Gideon Dragstorm, come to me,
Live your life beneath the sea.
You'll love it here with all these fish
And with those horns you're a total dish.

The singing was out of tune and the lyrics were ridiculous. Things didn't improve with the next verse.

No need for fear, no need to fret
You're a handsome faun, don't forget.

Who needs a normal boy or girl,

When you could be with this mermaid, Pearl?

Despite the terrible singing, Alice found herself smiling. The song made her feel warm and happy. Everyone else must have felt the same, because dreamy smiles had formed on their faces. Even Teddy's dripping jowls seemed to be grinning.

Dragstorm, meanwhile, was pulling off his expensive leather shoes. He scrambled down the rock face, his hooves negotiating the sheer cliff. He'd only got halfway down when he threw himself into the waves. As he swam through the water, Alice thought he was heading for them, but he swam past as if he didn't even notice them, a blissful look in his eyes.

'Way to go, Pearl!' hooted Miss Pinky.

'What's going on?' Alice asked as Medusa swam

closer to her.

'It's the mermaid's song,' said Medusa. 'Even the bad ones are impossible to resist if you're their intended victim. It's a mermaid's greatest power and Pearl has not let us down. Now swim for the shore.'

Alice looked up, expecting the fixies to attack, but instead they'd retreated higher in the sky, awaiting their master's command.

Whilst everyone dragged themselves on to the beach, gasping for breath, the singing stopped. Alice wiped the water from her eyes and scanned the waves, but there was no sign of Dragstorm.

'What has she done with him?' she asked Medusa, who was shaking water from her snakes whilst helping Polyphemus up the beach.

'She's not done anything to him,' cried Miss Pinky. 'Look!'

Kevin the kelpie was powering towards the beach

with a bedraggled, dripping Dragstorm stuck firmly to his back.

Alice pulled herself to her feet and pushed her dripping hair – or what was left of it after her close encounter with the fixie – out of her face.

'Hello, Minister,' she said, as the kelpie trotted over the pebbles. 'Enjoyed the ride?'

Dragstorm snarled as he shook a crab off one of his horns. His hair was so wet the curls stuck flat to his head. 'You pathetic monsters. It'll take more than mermaid music to stop me.'

'Mate,' said Miss Pinky, 'have you seen yourself? I'd say Pearl's performance reeled you right in, like a worm on a fishing line.'

'It did,' said Kevin in his deep voice. 'He'd have swum to his death had I not been waiting to intercept him.'

Dragstorm laughed. 'Ha! Like I'm supposed to be

grateful to a kid-killing kelpie like you!'

Kevin whinnied and flared his nostrils. 'How dare you!' he roared, raising himself up on his hind legs, before crashing down again like an angry stallion at the rodeo. He repeated this action, showering everyone with sea water, trying to throw off his glued-on rider.

On the fifth buck, the minister came unstuck, flying off and landing squarely on his hooves. Sneering, he straightened out his soaked suit and clicked his fingers. The fixies swarmed back down, taking up a V-shaped formation.

'You will not get away with any of this,' said Medusa calmly. 'The monster world will not stand for it.'

Dragstorm smiled. His bleached teeth hadn't suffered from his near-drowning. 'Monsters will be quaking on their claws when they hear how I beat a Category Five monster like this cyclops. But when they hear about how I saw off a Category Six monster too, they'll be as petrified as if you eye-blasted them yourself, Medusa.'

Alice looked at Dragstorm. How had this little snotty-nosed faun come so close to bringing monster world to disaster? 'I'm not sure your plan for monster domination is going that well,' she said.

'Be quiet, you ridiculous human,' snapped Dragstorm.

'Hey!' shouted Miss Pinky. 'Don't be nasty about humans. One of my best friends is one!'

'Yeah,' said Alice, 'and you can stop being mean to my monster friends, too.'

'Says who?' mocked Dragstorm.

'Says all of us!' boomed Polyphemus.

'Hear, hear!' chirped Fergus from somewhere, whilst Medusa applauded, and Teddy barked a deep and intestine-curdling bark.

'Shall I tell him, Medusa, or do you want to?' asked Alice.

'Tell me what?' said Dragstorm.

Medusa stepped forward. 'You are in no position to harm any of us.' She leaned in to within a few centimetres of Dragstorm's nose and tapped her glasses. 'Take a look, Minister: what do you see?

Dragstorm rolled his eyes and made a show of looking at himself in Medusa's mirrored sunglasses. 'I see nothing apart from my own handsome self.'

'Precisely,' said Medusa. 'You've lost your sunglasses.'

Dragstorm blinked, the colour draining from his cheeks. Then he composed himself. 'No matter,' he said, clicking his fingers. The fixies buzzed and grated their razor-sharp spurs together, then began to dive.

Raising her satchel above her head to shield herself from the aerial attack, Alice heard a loud squawk over the noise of the wind. Daring to peer up, she caught sight of a blur of silver-grey swooping in from over the sea. A huge griffin, larger even than Gordon, screeched as it veered towards the fixies, snapping and clawing at them, sending them tumbling in all directions with every beat of its wings.

Alice was too amazed to speak, but Medusa pulled herself up to her full height in front of Dragstorm. 'Where were we?' she asked quietly.

The minister stamped a hoof. 'No!' He glared at everyone. 'I will not allow a bunch of miserable monsters to defea—'

There was a flash of green and mid-rant Gideon Dragstorm turned from red-faced faun to stone-faced statue, his face contorted with rage.

Alice was frozen to the spot too, mouth open,

not quite believing what she was seeing. 'What have you done?'

'I did nothing!' Medusa cried out, quickly covering her eyes. 'I did not touch my glasses.'

'But look at him,' said Alice. 'You must have done it.'

'What is it?' boomed Polyphemus, confused. 'What has happened?'

'Looks like your wife has petrified the Minister for Monsters,' said Miss Pinky. 'And he's never looked better!'

'But I tell you it **wasn't me!**' Medusa sobbed, hands over her eyes.

As Alice stared in disbelief at the statue, a ghostly green figure shimmered into view, perched on Dragstorm's shoulder. He spun Medusa's sunglasses around on his finger.

'Lovely evening,' said Fergus, 'don't you think?'

'Oi! Bogey chops!' shouted Miss Pinky. 'Have you been geisting around?'

'I might have,' said Fergus. He flew over to Medusa and put the sunglasses back on.

'You!' screamed Medusa,

suddenly realising what had happened. '*You* removed my sunglasses?'

Fergus shrugged. 'He was getting on my nerves.'

'He was getting on all our nerves,' said Alice, 'but I'm not sure even he deserved to end up like this.'

'I am forbidden to use my powers,' said Medusa, whose snakes were whipping around manically. 'I will be sent to MonsterMax for this.'

'I'll tell them it was my fault,' said Fergus, solemnly. 'They can lock me up instead. I'm used to being in prison.'

Alice was about to walk over to examine the newly created statue when Miss Pinky screamed. 'Incoming!'

Everyone ran for cover as the griffin that had saved them from the fixies came in to land. From behind a rock, Alice watched as the creature swerved through the air, talons dropped, wings beating to steady itself as it approached. It hung just above the ground for a moment, then touched down perfectly. As the griffin drew in its enormous wings, the tip of its right one brushed against a stone horn on Dragstorm's head. The statue wobbled, once, twice, three times. But then gravity won the day. It fell to the side, smashing into dust, which the wind instantly picked up and blew across the beach and out to sea.

'Hello, everyone!'

'Uncle Magnus!' cried Alice, rushing over to the griffin's side. Magnus bent down to ruffle her hair. His own looked like it had been backcombed by a banshee. 'What are you doing here?' she asked.

'I couldn't just sit around doing nothing,' explained Magnus, 'so I had one of the stable hands saddle up a spare griffin. And just as well I did – those were some mean fixies!' He laughed and looked at the assembled escape team. 'Wow,' he said. 'I've clearly got some catching up to do.'

Miss Pinky skipped over, whiskers twitching. 'You won't believe the epic time we've had,' she said, jumping around on her paws. 'Alice is a star, *and* she's got superhero superpowers, *and* she's a hellhound whisperer, *and*—'

'And nothing,' said Alice. 'We've got Polyphemus back. That's all that matters.'

Magnus beamed at her. 'I knew you would,' he said. He looked around the crowd again. 'Someone's missing,' he said. 'I could have sworn I spotted Dragstorm.'

'You did,' said Medusa. 'It was he who kidnapped my husband.'

'Where is he?'

Alice bit her lip. Should they tell him or not?

'Well,' said Miss Pinky, 'he had a smashing time, didn't he, Alice?'

Alice looked at Miss Pinky and giggled. 'Yes,' she said, 'and then he kind of . . . cracked . . . under pressure!'

20. THIS IS ME!

Back at Jobs4Monsters, the rest of the week whizzed by in a blur of activity. Alice was kept busy answering the phone, booking interviews and tidying up after clients – including a rabble of squabbling cherubs who insisted on pulling each other's nappies off. At least four times a day she found herself in the staff toilet, mopping up after Fergus. The poltergeist had moved into the stationery cupboard, but he'd also discovered the joys of diving round the toilet's U-bend. Since their watery escape, he'd learned how to swim.

In any spare moments, Alice checked the Weird

Wild Web for updates from Medusa. There hadn't been much time on the island for proper goodbyes, but she had promised to stay in touch. So far, her updates had confirmed that the baby kraken had been reunited with its mother, though apparently it had been reluctant to give up its selkie toys and had had to be bribed with beach balls and a giant inflatable flamingo.

Medusa had also messaged to say that the remaining ghouls had been carted away to MonsterMax and that Teddy had been officially adopted at Balmoral. Everyone loved him, apart from Mrs Stuart, who had tried to feed him some of her mashed sprouts. 'She won't be doing that again!' wrote Medusa. As for Polyphemus, there were several snaps of him on Monstagram gleefully kneading, rolling and baking in the castle kitchen.

It wasn't until Friday morning that Alice noticed

the photo of Gideon Dragstorm was still on the office wall.

'I wonder whose photo we'll be putting up next,' said Miss Pinky, as she took it down. 'Maybe you should apply,' she said to Magnus, who was busy plumping the cushions on the new office sofa.

'No thanks!' he laughed. 'I have enough trouble dealing with the monsters we have here.'

Just before lunchtime, there was a knock at the door and a short, young man in royal livery and riding boots walked in. He had a long nose and pointy ears which poked out from his helmet. Alice guessed he was a goblin like Mrs Stuart, but without any of the housekeeper's rudeness.

'Can't stay long,' he said, smiling. 'I parked Gordon behind some wheelie bins. His wing is doing much better but I don't want to tire him out!' He held out a package and an envelope. 'Express delivery for

Alice MacAlister.'

Alice didn't need to open the package to know exactly what was inside. The mouth-watering aroma of salty cheese and pastry oozed through the wrapping.

'Wow!' Miss Pinky jumped up from her chair. 'Is that from Their Majesties?'

Alice looked at the flowing, curling handwriting; the ends of each letter coiled, like snakes, across the envelope. 'No. I don't think so.'

The goblin cleared his throat. 'Medusa sends her apologies for not coming in person. The Royal Bake Off has begun, and she is assisting her husband. When I left, they were up to forty-three layers of filo pastry, almost a record. The Spanish royal chef had just been disqualified for using shop-bought shortcrust, and the Norwegians were in full meltdown. It's pretty exciting.'

'Sounds it,' said Alice, trying to picture Polyphemus's giant, fat-fingered hands creating delicate pastries.

As soon as the goblin had left, Miss Pinky began hopping up and down with her tongue hanging out. 'What is it? What is it?'

'I think,' said Alice, 'it's Polyphemus's famous *spanakopita*.'

'I've never tried a spanky octopus,' said Miss Pinky.

Alice laughed and carefully unwrapped the package. Inside it was a huge slab of flaky, golden pastry, oozing with cheese. She set it on Miss Pinky's desk.

'Yummo!' Miss Pinky's whiskers hovered about a centimetre away from it. She licked her lips. 'Are you going to share it?'

'I think we should let Alice read her letter first,

don't you?' said Magnus.

Alice slipped the envelope into her pocket. 'It's OK. I'll read it later.' She wanted to read it in private anyway. 'I can't wait to taste it.'

Having eaten a thick wedge of the utterly delicious pastry, Alice left Magnus and Miss Pinky to fight over the last crumbs. She checked that Fergus wasn't playing in the plumbing and locked herself into the toilet to read the letter.

Alice took a deep breath before opening the envelope. She'd been hoping that Medusa would write to her. The gorgon had wanted to say something before they left the island, but there hadn't been time, and Alice had so many questions herself. Unfortunately, as she carefully unfolded the letter, she realised none of them were going to be answered.

Dear Alice,

Never doubt yourself.
Trust your instincts.

Your eternal friend, Medusa.

PS: Talk to Magnus. He, more than anyone, will understand.

Alice read the letter several times, but she still wasn't sure what to make of it. It was cryptic and mysterious, just like Medusa herself.

Alice folded the letter away. She thought for a moment about what her uncle could possibly understand more than anyone else and her tummy started turning somersaults. She hurried out into the office to find something to distract her from her thoughts.

She found jobs to do for the rest of the day, and before she knew it, Magnus said it was closing time.

'Promise you'll come back next school holidays,' begged Miss Pinky.

'I don't know what my mum will say,' said Alice, 'but I'd love to.'

Magnus winked. 'We'll find a way.'

Miss Pinky then presented Alice with a giant love heart card, covered in three glittery red letters.

'*BFF*,' read Alice. 'Best friends forever! That's lovely.'

'No.' Miss Pinky smiled, her whiskers twitching. 'Bravest Friends Forever!'

Before heading back to his flat for their final evening, Magnus took Alice up to Monsters' Munch for one of Doogie's special hotto choccos and some cake. They sat in the window and Alice glanced out at the passing pedestrians. *All these people*, thought Alice, *and none of them know about monsters.* Hopefully, Magnus, Miss Pinky and all the other amazing creatures out there would be able to keep it that way. She definitely wouldn't be telling anyone. Even if she was allowed, where would she start?

Magnus nudged her. 'There's something on your mind, isn't there?'

Alice couldn't bring herself to say it. It was a shame her uncle didn't have Medusa's mind-reading skills.

'You can ask me anything,' he said.

Alice looked at Magnus. In the café's lights, his eyes gleamed just like a wolf's. She thought about

Medusa's words: *Never doubt yourself. Trust your instincts.*

Then, with her heart pounding in her chest and her palms sweating, Alice looked around to make sure nobody could hear. 'When did you know that you were a werewolf?' she asked.

'About your age, I suppose,' said Magnus. 'I'd always had amazing hearing, but then I started getting these twinges at full moon. They started getting stronger until one day—'

'You transformed.'

Magnus looked at her. 'Exactly.'

'So, Mum knows about all this?' Then Alice suddenly gasped. 'She's not a werewolf too, is she?'

'No,' said Magnus, smiling. 'But you're right – she does know about me. It was kind of hard to hide when we were growing up. In fact, she used to remind me when it was a full moon. I've always been a bit rubbish remembering to take my antidote. She knows the werewolf gene is in the family. But of course, she couldn't say anything to you.'

'It's the monster law,' said Alice. 'I know.'

Magnus reached for her hand. 'I think it's why she kept you away from dogs – in case you discovered you could talk to them before you were old enough to understand why. You said they kept trying to get in your pram when you were a baby, didn't you?'

Alice nodded.

'They probably sensed something special about you, even then.'

Alice took a sip of her hot chocolate. 'At least I know why Mum has never let me eat meat,' she said. 'She's scared that I might get a real taste for it, isn't she?'

'I expect so,' said Magnus. 'But she's only been trying to protect you. Just in case.'

'Just in case what?' asked Alice.

'In case you turned out like me,' said Magnus.

Alice thought about this for a moment. 'There's nothing wrong with you,' she said.

Magnus smiled at her. 'There's nothing wrong with you either. And there's plenty of time to get used to the idea. That's what you really wanted to know, isn't it?'

Alice nodded. The clues all added up: her keen sense of smell; the lick pad that had let her into Jobs4Monsters; that weird shiver she'd felt on the night when Magnus transformed; Teddy being able to understand her. Plus, most important of all, the fact she felt so at home with her new monster friends.

'I'm a werewolf!' she burst out, finally saying the words she'd been thinking for days.

'Yes,' said Magnus. 'You are.' He squeezed her hand tightly. 'But there's nothing to be scared about.'

Alice took a deep breath. *Am I scared?* she asked herself. Her spine was tingling, and her skin was prickling. But it wasn't like the terror she'd felt when the kraken lassoed her ankle and dragged her to the pool. It was more like the feeling she'd had when she first discovered this world of monsters.

'It's OK,' she said. 'I'm not scared. Maybe a bit nervous, but mostly I'm excited. And there's tons of things I don't know. Do I have to register with the ministry? Will I have to go to special monster school? What happens next?' She looked at Magnus expectantly.

'Next, you're going home to tell your mum,' he said. 'Everything else can wait till you come back to visit us. There's no hurry.' Magnus stared at her with a concerned look in his eyes. 'You will come back, won't you?'

Alice didn't even need to think about it. 'Try and

stop me!' she said, grinning. 'I'm a monster, aren't I?
This is where I belong!'

Acknowledgements

Monster-sized thanks to:

Thérèse Coen, agent *par excellence*, and fierce fan of my monsters.

My fiendishly brilliant editors, Anne Marie Ryan and Sarah Leonard.

Kim Geyer, whose sensational illustrations make me howl with delight.

The whole team at Orchard, who have helped my monsters run, fly, swim and crawl across the pages of this book.

My friends at the Society of Children's Book Writers & Illustrators, for your support and encouragement as I've clawed my way to publication.

The folk at Floris Books and the Kelpies Prize, for roaring approval early on.

Special thanks to my mum, who is not a monster, but who put up with me when I was.

And to Andrew, for laughing at life and finding the funny with me every day, and for holding my hand through the scary bits.

JUSTIN DAVIES WWW.JUSTINDAVIESAUTHOR.COM

Like all superheroes, Justin leads a double life. In one, he flies around the world in his job as cabin crew, visiting all the places he found in his atlas as a boy. In his other life, Justin lives with his husband and writes books which he hopes will make you laugh. Although he doesn't have super-smellability like Alice, he can sniff out the best bakery anywhere he goes!

KiM GEYER WWW.KIMGEYER.COM

Kim designed textiles before taking up her drawing pencil to illustrate well-dressed characters in children's books. She lives and works in London with a brood of her very own monsters and a giant cactus called Benedict.